"This house [...] touch..."

Jane put Mercy into her bouncy seat. "There, *liebling*."

"Was she good this morning?"

"Like gold. She's such a sweet baby."

Levy closed his eyes for a silent prayer, then swallowed a spoonful. "It was *Gott*'s will you got stranded at that train station. Already I don't know what I'd do without you."

For just a moment, Jane's heart gave a thump. Whatever happened, she wouldn't let herself become attracted to Levy. "I'm grateful for the job." Her remark was deliberate, to remind Levy she worked for him and nothing else.

"Mercy seems happy, too." He toyed with the baby's feet, encased in thin flannel socks. "Maybe she knows she's no longer subject to a fumbling bachelor's care."

"Why..." Jane stopped.

"Why what?"

"Nothing." She'd almost asked him why he wasn't married.

It was none of her business. If she didn't want him prying into her past, she had no right to pry into his...

Living on a remote self-sufficient homestead in North Idaho, **Patrice Lewis** is a Christian wife, mother, author, blogger, columnist and speaker. She has practiced and written about rural subjects for almost thirty years. When she isn't writing, Patrice enjoys self-sufficiency projects, such as animal husbandry, small-scale dairy production, gardening, food preservation and canning, and homeschooling. She and her husband have been married since 1990 and have two daughters.

Books by Patrice Lewis

Love Inspired

The Amish Newcomer
Amish Baby Lessons

Visit the Author Profile page at Harlequin.com.

Having then gifts differing
according to the grace that is given to us,
whether prophecy, let us prophesy
according to the proportion of faith;

Or ministry, let us wait on our ministering:
or he that teacheth, on teaching;

Or he that exhorteth, on exhortation:
he that giveth, let him do it with simplicity;
he that ruleth, with diligence;
he that sheweth mercy, with cheerfulness.
—*Romans* 12:6–8

To God, for blessing me
with my husband and daughters,
the best family anyone could hope for.

Chapter One

A crowd of people swirled around her on the hot train platform in Lafayette, Indiana, but Jane Troyer ignored them. The station was busy, with garbled announcements made over distant loudspeakers and the din of hundreds of passengers. Her head ached from the chaos. She sat alone on a bench next to her suitcase, trying not to give in to despair.

Running away from heartbreak was turning out to be harder than she'd thought. Moving to another town to live with her aunt and uncle had seemed like an easy solution. Until...

"*Geht es dir gut*? Are you all right?"

She lifted her head and saw a man in Amish suspenders and a straw hat, with a bag slung over one shoulder and a fractious baby in his arms. A streak of sweat ran down one temple and his blue eyes looked weary.

"*Nein*, I'm not," she replied. "Someone just stole my bag with all my money in it. I'm stranded here." She wondered why *Gott* had deserted her at this strange train station.

He bounced the baby. "Where are you going?"

"To visit my aunt and uncle in Grand Creek. It's about twenty miles away."

"I live in Grand Creek. Who are your aunt and uncle?"

"Peter and Catherine Troyer. They run a dry-goods store, a mercantile, in the center of town."

"They're practically my neighbors!" The man smiled. "I'd be happy to take you there." He swayed the baby in his arms.

"Will you?" She jumped up from the bench. "*Danke! Danke!*"

"You're welcome. But first I have some things to collect here at the station, some boxes." The baby gave a wail, and he grimaced. "They're large boxes too."

"Why are you picking up large boxes with a *boppli* in tow? That doesn't make sense." He seemed like he didn't know how to handle a baby. The baby seemed to know it too.

"Because there was no one to watch her. And I need the boxes. They're part of my business."

"Would it help if I held the *boppli*? That would free your hands."

Despite the infant's crankiness, the man seemed reluctant to relinquish his burden. "I wouldn't do that to you. She's irritable. She hasn't calmed down all day." As if to reinforce his words, the baby wailed, tears streaming down her face.

"That's okay. I don't mind." She reached for the child.

"Well, if you're sure…" He transferred the baby to

her. "I hope you don't regret it. I'll be back in a few minutes."

Jane accepted the warm little bundle and cooed at the child. "Hush, hush…"

As the baby quieted, Jane looked up in time to see the man's jaw drop. He snapped his mouth shut. "I've never seen her calm down that fast," he said in wonder.

"It's a gift *Gott* gave me." Jane shoved her eyeglasses higher on her nose. "Why don't I stay here while you get your boxes? That way I can make sure some other *Englischer* doesn't run away with my suitcase too."

"*Ja.* Here's her diaper bag." He removed the strap from his shoulder and dropped the bag on the bench. "I won't be long."

Jane sat down. She wondered why the man didn't have a beard. All Amish men grew their beards once they married, and certainly by the time babies came. And why was he trying to juggle an infant at the same time he was picking up large boxes from a train station? Why wasn't his wife caring for the child? She shook her head. None of it made sense.

The infant in her arms had large blue eyes, the wrinkled lids showing her to be very young, perhaps no more than a couple weeks old. At a time when most of her friends were married and starting families, Jane's arms had ached to hold her own baby, but that wasn't likely to happen anytime soon.

This visit to her aunt and uncle was to help her mend her broken heart. Her best friend had married the man Jane had spent so many years loving from afar. She didn't blame Isaac for never noticing her. Most men didn't. But it still hurt. Why had *Gott* made her so plain? She blinked back tears of self-pity.

Her mother always told her she made up for her lack of beauty with an abundance of character, but that was small comfort as her friends, one by one, settled into marital bliss, leaving her the sole unmarried woman from among her cohorts.

Her older sister Elizabeth, married now, was the beauty of the family. It was hard growing up in her shadow, even though her sister's character was just as lovely as her face. But Jane—who needed to wear glasses from a young age, then grew lanky and tall— felt awkward by comparison. Except when it came to babies. For whatever reason, her confidence soared with a baby in her arms.

The ironic thing was she was unlikely to ever have babies of her own. Marriage just didn't seem to be *Gott*'s plan for her.

The baby currently in her arms crinkled her face and started to wail again. Jane guessed she was hungry. "Where's your *mamm*?" she asked. Jane tried soothing the infant, but the *boppli* only wailed louder.

In desperation, Jane rummaged through the diaper bag and found two bottles.

Jane removed one, popped off the cap and determined it was the right temperature. She inserted the tip into the baby's mouth. The *boppli* immediately stopped crying and started suckling. A little piece of Jane's heart melted as she cuddled the infant.

"*Gut*, you found the bottles."

Jane looked up. The man hurried toward her, beads

of sweat trickling down one side of his face. He was
taller than her by several inches, which put him near six
feet in height. He had the strapping look of a hardworking farmer. His dark blue shirt, damp from humidity,
mirrored the dark blue of his eyes. But it still puzzled
her why he had no beard. Married men grew beards.

"I loaded the boxes as fast as I could. Sorry to take
so long…" he continued.

"Don't worry about it. I found everything I needed
in the diaper bag. But now you'll have to wait until she
finishes eating."

"That's fine." He sat down on the bench. "*Ach*, what a
day it's been so far." He heaved out an enormous breath.

"Bad day?" She shifted the infant. Her own trou-
bles were forgotten for a moment as her curiosity got
the better of her.

"You don't know the half of it. I'm grateful you
minded the *boppli* while I collected my boxes." He
fished a bandanna out of his pocket and mopped his
face. "*Ach*, it's warm for this early in July."

"She's a *gut* baby," she offered. "No trouble at all."

"For you, maybe. For me, she's been nothing *but*
trouble."

"My name is Jane Troyer, by the way."

"Levy Struder. The baby's name is Mercy."

"Oh, that's lovely." She smiled at the infant, whose
eyes were half-closed as she concentrated on drinking
her bottle.

"And apt. She needs all *Gott*'s mercy she can get."

Jane didn't ask for an explanation, but she put two

and two together. Could Levy be widowed? He didn't act like a grieving man, but he *did* look like a harried one.

The baby pulled away from the bottle at last, so Jane took a clean cloth diaper from the bag and put it over her shoulder. She hitched up the infant over the cloth and patted her back. "I think she's ready to go."

"*Ja*. I'll take your suitcase. My buggy is this way."

Jane patted little Mercy's back until she heard a delicate *braaap*, then kept the baby there as she followed Levy toward a hitching post in the shade of a tree where a dozing horse stood hitched to a buggy.

He swung her suitcase into the back of the buggy, on top of a large number of big cardboard boxes. "I'll hold the baby while you get in."

She handed over the drowsy child. A large basket, padded with soft blankets as an impromptu cradle, occupied the seat. She moved it toward the back, climbed in and took the baby in her arms. Levy unhitched the horse, gave it a pat on the neck and climbed in beside her. He clucked, and the horse trotted out of the train station's parking lot.

"Ah, it's good to get away from there." Jane leaned back in the seat and cuddled the infant close to her chest. "It's been a long trip, and I don't like being among so many strangers." The horse pulled them through busy streets, laden with cars and stoplights and noise.

"You said you were robbed? What a bad start to your visit. How much money got stolen?"

"I had about fifty dollars in my bag." Her face hardened. "It was all I had."

"Did you report it to the station manager?"

"No. What could he do? The thief snatched my bag out of my hand and disappeared. By the time I would have found the station manager, my money would be far away."

"Did he steal anything else?"

"Just a handkerchief."

"There's a spare in the diaper bag if you need one." Humor crinkled his eyes. "I wonder if the thief was disappointed in getting only a handkerchief."

"Serves him right." Seeing the lighter side, Jane chuckled. "At least it was clean."

Levy guided the horse away from the station. "It will take about two hours to get to Grand Creek," he warned. "I try not to make this trip any more often than I have to. I can't tell you how hard it was, driving here with Mercy in a basket."

"Why didn't you leave her with someone?" She paused, then decided to probe a bit. "Your wife?"

"I'm not married. This is my niece."

"Oh. I see."

She saw his mouth tighten, but he didn't explain why he was caring for his newborn niece, and she didn't ask where the baby's mother was.

"I had a *youngie* watching her," he explained, "but she's inexperienced with babies, and she was busy today anyway, just when I needed her most. I'm going to have to find someone more dependable."

"*Ach*, that's hard." She looked down at little Mercy in her arms. The warm bundle filled an empty hole in her heart, and she hugged the baby to herself. "Look, she's sleeping. She'll be quiet now the rest of the trip, I think."

Levy sighed. "I can't thank you enough. *Bopplin* are a lot harder than I thought."

"*Ja.*" If this was his niece, why was he taking care of his sibling's child? There was some sort of mystery here.

He set the horse at a comfortable trot as the town fell behind them. He took a side road filled with rolling hills and broad farms. A slight breeze cooled the heat.

"So—what brings you here to visit your aunt and uncle?" inquired Levy. "Where are you from? Are you staying long with them?"

Jane took a moment before answering. She didn't want to start explaining why she'd taken such an extended trip or what she left behind. Now was not the time to explain her mixed-up love life.

"I'm from Jasper, Ohio," she answered. "It's about a four-hour train ride from here. I told Onkel Peter I'd be happy to work in the store. He said he could use another clerk, and offered me a job." Anxious to avoid delving into her background, she changed the subject. "What is it you do?"

"Produce farming, with some accounting on the side. The boxes I picked up at the station hold crates and display materials for weekend sales at a farmer's market where I sell every Saturday through the end of October. Nearly all my yearly income is earned during the summer at the farmer's market, so it's a very busy time for me. As you can imagine, taking care of Mercy is going to be difficult."

Jane's brow furrowed. "Why are you taking care of her at all, if she's your niece?"

"Because my sister isn't here." His words were clipped.

All kinds of questions floated around in Jane's mind. If his sister wasn't here, what about the baby's father? Was the infant an orphan? It seemed Levy was being just as cagey about why he was caring for a young infant as she was in relating her reasons for leaving her hometown. "She's a beautiful baby" was all she said.

"Yes, she is. And she deserves more than being cared for by a bachelor uncle."

"Why haven't you asked someone to help you? The community must be full of women who would be happy to lend a hand."

"I… I've only had her a few days. The *youngie* I hired doesn't seem to be comfortable with an infant this young. I'm going to have to find someone more experienced." He gave her a sidelong look, then turned his attention back to the horse. The animal's hooves clattered in a comfortable rhythm.

Jane didn't ask the circumstances under which little Mercy was dropped in her uncle's lap. She would hear it soon enough. "*Ja*, it's unusual for a man to take care of a baby all on his own."

"It also gives me a new appreciation for young mothers." He steadied the horse as a car passed. "You're not married?"

"N-no." She kept her expression neutral. She had no intention of explaining herself. "I'd rather not discuss it."

His eyebrows rose. "Is there a story there?"

"If there is, it's none of your business."

"If you say so." He grinned, and Jane caught her breath. She didn't want to encourage any flirting. It made her uneasy. In her twenty-three years, she'd learned men didn't flirt with her. Men didn't court her. Men hardly paid attention to her at all—except to see her as a *useful* person, a woman willing to work hard. A woman willing to tackle difficult chores. It seemed to be her role in life.

She shoved her glasses back up her nose. "You're rude, Mr. Struder."

"And you're a mystery, Miss Troyer."

She hugged the baby closer, feeling as if the infant was a defense against unwelcome assumptions by Levy Struder. The unasked question hovered in the air—*Why don't you have any of your own?*—and she was grateful Levy didn't voice it. Instead, she turned the tables. "Mercy must have caused you quite a flurry of preparations, if she came to you unexpectedly."

"*Ja*, she did. I had nothing for a baby. It's hard to get work done. I tried bringing her out into the fields with me in her basket, but that only lasted a few minutes at a time. I didn't realize how demanding young babies are. Or how much women do to care for them."

"That's our secret weapon," joked Jane. "We make it seem easy."

By the time they approached Grand Creek, Jane was glad to see the familiar green fields, produce stands and white farmhouses of an Amish community. Mercy woke up and whimpered briefly, but she settled into Jane's arms and seemed content to be held.

"I've never seen her so quiet." Levy waved at a distant acquaintance as they passed by on the road. "She's been fussy since she came to me. Frankly, I was just about at my wit's end."

"At this age, babies are pretty simple creatures," replied Jane. "Food, clean diapers, close body contact. That's about it."

"I think it's a woman's touch too. She didn't seem too happy to have me hold her."

"Maybe you need baby lessons." She smiled at the thought of teaching this strange man how to care for an infant. Caring for babies came to her so naturally that even this unfamiliar baby lay content in her arms. It was ironic that *Gott* would grant her the gift of soothing babies, but very little likelihood she would ever have any of her own.

"Baby lessons. Maybe I do need them—" He interrupted himself, "Look! See that building over there?" He pointed to a large squat brick commercial building with a broad front porch at the town's crossroad. Colorful cloth swagging swooped between the porch columns, lending the building an air of festivity. "That's your aunt and uncle's store. But it's late, and they're closed. I'll take you straight to their house, if you like. It's not far."

"I'm just glad to see horses and buggies again." She gazed around at the wide, quiet streets arced over by generous shade trees. As they approached the far edge of town, lots gave way to small farms between five and fifteen acres.

"You said you came from Ohio? Does it have *Englischers*? How many people live there in your town?"

"I'm guessing Jasper has five thousand people or so." She shoved her glasses up her nose. "Ohio is pretty crowded. This town seems smaller and more rural. I like seeing all these small farms. It seems things are spread out a bit more here in Indiana."

"Grand Creek has about two thousand people. I live on the outskirts, that way." He gestured. "Near your aunt and uncle."

"And you live by yourself?"

"*Ja.* I, uh… I do now."

Jane noticed his hesitation. Was he referencing his sister? She wondered at the secrecy.

Yet it was none of her business. She was here to heal, to work, to be useful—not to get involved in a stranger's problems. Starting over in a new town was better than stewing in heartbreak and unrequited love.

Soon a white two-story clapboard house came into view. It was set back from the road and shaded by huge maples, with generous front and back porches. "That's where you're going." Levy pointed. "There's your uncle in the yard, mowing the grass."

She peered through the late-afternoon sunshine and saw her uncle's light blue shirt. His hair and long beard were grayer than she remembered.

"I haven't seen him in years!" Jane couldn't keep the excitement out of her voice. "The last time I saw Onkel Peter and Tante Catherine was three years ago, when my sister Elizabeth got married."

Levy turned the horse into the drive. "Everyone likes them, and their dry-goods mercantile does very well."

"Onkel Peter! Onkel Peter!" Jane waved.

Her uncle paused in his mowing and squinted. "Jane? Child, I thought you were coming by taxi."

"I was. Then an *Englischer* stole my money. This man, Levy, he found me and brought me along."

"*Ja*, I see that." Her uncle smiled. "*Vielen Dank*, Levy."

"Here, put the baby in the basket." Levy dragged the lined basket up front.

Jane laid the infant in the makeshift cradle. The child whimpered. "She might need her diaper changed," she warned Levy, who looked uncomfortable being in sole charge of the baby once more. Then she jumped out of the buggy and embraced her uncle.

"Your aunt will be very happy you're here," said Peter. "She's been talking nonstop about your visit."

But Jane was watching Levy. "Will you be okay?" she asked him.

"I'll be okay." He clucked to Maggie, the horse. "I hope!"

Jane heard Mercy's wailing as he drove away. She shook her head. "He's in trouble," she muttered.

Levy tried to ignore little Mercy's cries from her basket. The familiar tension and sense of helplessness enveloped him, as it had since the baby was metaphorically and literally dumped in his lap.

In contrast to his incompetence, this unknown woman, Jane Troyer, had an amazing ability when it came to soothing the infant.

What an odd package she was. Mousy brown hair, large glasses and amazing huge blue eyes. She was not beautiful, but there was something about her that piqued his interest. Her astounding aptitude with Mercy showed a maternal instinct he admired. Certainly she had more instinct than his sister Eliza had.

He compressed his lips. What was Eliza thinking, to send such a tiny infant to him? Did she think he was qualified to raise his niece, especially after the mess he'd made raising his own sister?

He hadn't asked to step into the role of surrogate father to his only sibling. But when his parents were killed in a buggy accident when he was eighteen, he'd thought himself capable of reining in a rebellious twelve-year-old sister.

He was wrong.

"*Gott*, forgive me," he whispered. Whether he required forgiveness for his thoughts about his sister, or his failure to raise her properly, it was lost in the anxiety of getting Mercy to stop crying.

He pulled Maggie, the horse, into the small barn and hopped out. Ignoring the squalling infant, he unharnessed the animal, led her into a stall, gave her a brief grooming, fed and watered her and opened the back stall door so she could access the adjacent pasture. Finally he collected the red-faced baby and diaper bag and headed into the house. By the time he sat in the rocking chair and got the baby to take a bottle, he was frazzled and exhausted.

Why had the young babysitter elected to bail on him today of all days?

He rocked the infant as she nursed, his thoughts racing through all the work he needed to get done, but couldn't. His income depended on selling his produce at the farmer's market, but he couldn't work if he had to care for Mercy. And if he couldn't depend on the teenage babysitter if she was going to flake on him when he needed her most. What could he do? He'd have to ask around to see who else might be available. Without finding Mercy a consistent caregiver, he couldn't work his farm, sell at the farmer's market, or do anything necessary to earn a living. A baby, he now realized, required almost constant care and attention.

His thoughts settled on Jane. She said she had a job at the Troyers' dry-goods store, but he wondered if she would be interested in taking care of Mercy instead.

It was worth asking her. No, it was worth *begging* her. He needed help. Now.

Chapter Two

Uncle Peter—a little more solid around the middle than last she saw him—picked up her suitcase and led the way into the house. "Sounds like you had quite an adventure."

"*Ja.* I'm glad to be here." She gazed after Levy's buggy as his horse trotted away. "But I'm worried about the baby."

"So are we. He just got her a few days ago. " Her uncle walked up the porch steps. "Come inside, your aunt is most anxious to see you."

Within moments Jane found herself enveloped in her aunt's embrace. "*Welkom! Welkom!*"

Jane hugged the woman hard and gave her a smacking kiss. "*Danke!* It's been so long."

Catherine's smoothed-back hair was still brown, but now laced with gray. Her blue eyes twinkled through the creases on her face. Motherly in the extreme, she insisted Jane sit and have tea and cookies.

Jane leaned back with a sigh. "*Ach,* it's good to be here. I'm grateful for the chance to get out of Jasper."

"It was that bad, then?"

"*Nein*, but it was getting…lonely. All my friends are married. Most already have babies. Hannah is expecting her first. *Mamm* thought I was becoming brittle. That's the term she used, brittle. She said my humor was getting sarcastic, and that would soon turn to bitterness. I had to ask myself, at what point do I give up and realize I have nothing in front of me? *Mamm* said I needed a change of scenery, so here I am."

Uncle Peter patted her hand before reaching for his mug of tea. "You're welcome to stay with us as long as you wish. With your cousins all out on their own, it will be nice to have a *youngie* in the house again. In the store too. We've been busy so far this summer."

"I'm looking forward to it. You'll have to teach me what to do, of course. My only job experience up to this point has been working with children, mostly babysitting."

"You always were *gut* with babies." Catherine chuckled. "I wonder if you shouldn't ask Levy whether he needs help. He's had a hard time coping, and the *youngie* he hired isn't very dependable."

"But what about the store? I don't want to leave you two in the lurch, since you're being kind enough to give me a place to live." Jane kept her voice casual. "Where's the baby's mother? Levy didn't go into any details."

Catherine exchanged a lightning glance with Peter. "I don't want to gossip, *liebling*, so that's a story you'll have to get directly from Levy."

"I'm a stranger, so I don't think he'll tell me. We only just met, after all."

"*Ja*, true." Peter stroked his beard. "But he's determined to raise the baby himself, which is causing all sorts of concern among the elders. The bishop tells him he should simply give the *boppli* to a family to raise."

"That makes sense," said Jane. "So what's the problem?"

"The problem is, he won't do it."

Jane raised her eyebrows. "He's going against the recommendation of the bishop?"

"*Ja.*" Peter looked troubled. "The bishop is looking at what's *gut* for the baby, but Levy insists his guardianship of the baby is only temporary and his sister will be back soon."

"I'm guessing Mercy was born out of wedlock?" It happened sometimes, Jane knew.

Catherine nodded and her eyes moistened. "We can only assume so. An *Englisch* woman knocked at Levy's door a couple days ago, handed him the baby and a note, then disappeared. The note only said the baby was Eliza's, but she was unable to care for her, so she wanted Levy to raise her since he was the one person she trusted above all others."

"Oh my." Jane whispered the words. "How sad." No wonder the man was at his wit's end.

"I know Levy blames himself for Eliza's behavior." Peter spoke into the poignant silence. "It's hard to watch him suffer, harder still to know what's happening with Eliza. I remember her as a sweet young woman. But after her parents died, she snapped. She became rebellious and fascinated with the *Englisch* world. Then one day she was gone. No one knows what happened to her, until suddenly a *boppli* shows up."

"It certainly puts things into perspective," ventured Jane. "What I left behind is nothing next to what Levy is facing."

"Jane." Catherine put down her mug of tea. "I know you're upset by what happened back home, when that man—what was his name, Isaac?—married your best friend. But you're here now. You can have a useful life with us."

Useful. Jane was coming to hate that term. It seemed being *useful* was all she was good for. "Of course, Tante." Useful, not pretty. Useful, not interesting. Useful, not marriageable. "But I do find it humiliating that Isaac never had eyes for me, only my best friend. Sometimes I get a little mad at *Gott* for making me so plain."

"*Liebling*, I don't think you're plain." Catherine looked troubled. "Besides, you know *Gott* sees what's on the inside, and someday you'll meet a man who sees that too. Have you prayed?"

"Of course. But if *Gott* has answered my prayers, I haven't noticed yet." The moment the words were out of her mouth, she felt ashamed. Her mother had warned her that her sharp tongue was changing from witty to harsh. "I'm sorry, Tante Catherine."

"*Gott* is bigger than us. I'm sure He understands being angry."

A clock chimed over the kitchen sink, and Catherine and Peter both glanced at it.

"The chores!" her uncle exclaimed. "I have to get to the milking."

"Can I help?"

"*Ja, danke.* Sometimes I get a little tired of doing the milking all by myself."

Jane rose from her seat.

"I'll take your suitcase upstairs." Catherine also stood up. "Go on, get the chores done and I'll have a nice meal ready when you're finished."

Jane followed her uncle and took a clean bucket from the kitchen counter, then strode behind him toward the small barn behind the house. "How many cows do you have?"

"Just three now. We're slowing down. How many does your father keep?"

"Ten, so milking three won't take long with both of us."

The doe-eyed Jerseys chewed their cud in the shade of a fine maple tree behind the barn. Clipping halters to lead ropes, Jane and her uncle led two of the animals inside and tied them to a rail. With an ease born of experience, she sat on a low crate and wiped down the animal's udder, then zinged the warm milk into the bucket.

"So Isaac got married, eh?" Uncle Peter asked as he began milking.

"*Ja.*" Jane sighed. "And I'll admit, I'm angry about it. To be fair, I don't think he ever knew I loved him. But it hurt when Hannah—my best friend—fell in love with him. It was too hard for me to be around them anymore. I had to leave."

"It sounds like you're angry with your friend Hannah. But no one understands the chemistry of the heart except *Gott*. Things will work out, *schätzchen*. Meanwhile, your aunt and I couldn't be happier to have you staying with us as long as you like."

With her forehead pressed against the cow's flank, she felt the pressure of tears at her uncle's kindness. "*Danke*, Onkel Peter. I'll help out every way I can."

"And I hope you'll have some fun too. There are many activities for the *youngies* around here. In fact, there's a barbecue this Friday evening, so you can start getting acquainted with people your age. Who knows, maybe…" He trailed off.

"Maybe *not*," she replied, following her uncle's unspoken wish that she might meet someone special. "Right now I don't want to meet anyone. I'd rather work in your store. That's all."

"Your time will come, child." Her uncle's words were gentle and teasing.

Jane felt better. "*Ja*, I know. Sometimes I just get impatient." She squeezed out the last few drops of milk. "Do you want me to get the other cow?"

"*Nein*, I'll finish up. You're probably tired after your journey anyway. Tell your aunt I'll be there in a few minutes."

Jane released the cow and seized the bucket filled with warm, foamy milk. The early July twilight enveloped her as she walked back to the house. She paused a moment to admire the tidy, widely spaced farmhouses set back from the gravel road with small holdings tucked in back. Crickets chirped from hidden ditches, and robins hopped along lawns and fence posts. She saw the familiar huge gardens and small fields of corn and oats.

In the large airy kitchen, Aunt Catherine took a bubbling casserole dish out of the oven. The rich smell of cheese filled the air.

"Macaroni and cheese!" exclaimed Jane. "You remembered!"

Catherine laughed. "Of course I remembered your favorite dish."

Jane knew the cheddar cheese was homemade from the output of the cows she'd helped milk. The top of the dish was crusty with a mixture of breadcrumbs and Parmesan cheese.

Jane set the bucket of fresh milk on the counter. "Show me around the kitchen so I know where everything is."

The spacious kitchen was painted in cheerful shades of sage and cream, with a large, solid table and six upright chairs dominating the center. Streams of evening light poured through the window over the sink. Her aunt opened cupboards and drawers until Jane was familiar with the layout. Uncle Peter came in and set two more buckets of milk on the counter. Catherine strained the milk through a clean cloth, then poured the milk into large jars and put them down in the cool cellar. Jane set the table.

After a silent blessing, Catherine dished up the food. Jane forked some pasta into her mouth. "Oh, Tante Catherine, no one makes this better than you."

Then she paused. From outside, she thought she heard the thin distant wail of a crying baby.

Peter cocked his head. "Is that…?"

Jane heard the wail grow louder, then a knock came at the kitchen door. Peter jumped up and answered it.

Levy stood on the small porch, looking harried. The

baby wailed in his arms. "*Gut'n owed*, Peter," said Levy politely. "Is your niece in?"

"*Ja. Komm* in." Peter stood aside as Jane rose to her feet.

Levy stepped into the kitchen. "*Gut'n owed*, Jane."

"*Gut'n owed*." She wiped her mouth and put the napkin on the table. "Is there something you need?"

"I need a nanny." His words were blunt and held a note of desperation.

She gaped. The poor man certainly looked stressed beyond belief, and Jane wondered if the infant had stopped crying since she last saw him.

"You need a nanny?" she parroted. "Now?"

"*Ja*, now. This instant. I can't seem to make her stop crying."

More from instinct than anything else, Jane reached for the child and cuddled her. "Shh, *liebling*, shhh…" She swayed the baby in her arms.

Within half a minute, the baby calmed down and fell into a peaceful silence.

She looked up and saw the same stunned expression on Levy's face he'd worn when she'd quieted the baby at the train station that afternoon.

He snapped his jaw closed. "How do you do it?" he asked in wonder. "I haven't been able to soothe her at all."

"I've always been able to calm babies," she replied simply. "I used to babysit all the time, and often mothers hired me to help when they had a newborn."

"Levy, we're just sitting down to eat dinner." Catherine pointed to an empty chair. "Have you eaten? You're welcome to join us."

"*Ja, danke*, I will. I've been too busy with the *boppli* to think about food."

Catherine fetched another plate and some cutlery, then dished up a portion of the casserole for Levy.

With the quiet baby in her arms, Jane sat back down. "You said you need a nanny, and I can understand why, but I came here to work in Onkel Peter's store."

"I know. But Peter—" he turned to the older man "—I'm in desperate need of help. You know how busy I am this time of year. I can't tend the garden or harvest crops or even sell at the farmer's market while caring for an infant."

"*Ja*, I see that. But the decision is Jane's."

Levy turned to her. "What do you say?"

Jane looked at the warm, trusting baby in her arms. The infant's eyelids drooped, and she seemed moments away from nodding off to sleep. "I think, if you can spare me from the store, I'd like to take care of her. She's a darling *boppli*. And maybe I can give Levy some baby lessons." She glanced at him.

"*Danke*." Levy looked relieved beyond words. "Later this evening, maybe you can come to the house and I'll show you around. *Danke*," he babbled again. "*Vielen Dank*."

Catherine chuckled. "Eat," she told him, "before the food gets cold."

When the meal was over, Jane rose to help with the dishes, but Catherine waved her off. "Why don't you go with Levy now and see what he needs you to do?"

"Actually, I've got the barn chores to do first." Levy stood up and placed his napkin on the table. He looked at Jane. "Can you give me half an hour or so?"

"*Ja*, sure. Do you want me to bring the baby with me? She's sleeping right now."

"*Nein*, if she's sleeping, I'll just lay her in her crib. Here, I'll take her."

Having seen his previous reaction to the infant, Jane considered it a minor miracle the infant didn't wake up when she transferred her to her uncle's arms. "First baby lesson," she told him. "Support her a bit more under the head, like this." She positioned his arm more securely around the baby.

"*Ja*, that feels better." He looked at the child, and for the first time Jane saw tenderness on his face toward his niece. He raised his head. "Half an hour then?"

"I'll be there."

"Catherine, *danke* for supper." He smiled. "I didn't realize how hungry I was."

Catherine flapped a hand. "Go on, now. It was nothing."

Cradling the infant, Levy touched the brim of his hat and departed.

"Whew." Jane sat down. "Looks like I have a job."

"The *boppli* needs you more than we do," affirmed Peter. "I think you made the right decision."

"Will this leave you in a lurch, since I was supposed to work in the store?"

"*Nein*, we'll be fine," said Catherine. "And your uncle is right. The *boppli* needs you. So does Levy." She chuckled.

"I offered to give him baby lessons," Jane commented. "Looks like that's what I'll be doing."

"He needs them, for sure and certain. *Nein, liebling,*

don't worry about dishes. Why don't you go unpack until it's time to go to Levy's? Your suitcase is upstairs, second bedroom on the left."

Jane climbed the stairs and found the bedroom, glowing and quiet as the late-evening sun streamed in the window. It was plainly furnished with a colorful quilt on the bed, a chest of drawers, a rocking chair and some hooks on the wall for clothing.

With one suitcase, it took her no time to unpack. Before heading back downstairs, Jane stepped into the bathroom to splash her face and tidy some stray wisps that had escaped her *kapp*. She gave herself one hard look in the mirror and turned away. She didn't like mirrors. It only reminded her of what she lacked.

In the kitchen, Aunt Catherine was just finishing the dishes. "I guess I'll be going. Where is Levy's house?"

Catherine wiped her hands on a dish towel, then pointed. "It's the little farm at the end of this road, maybe half a mile away. White house, big front porch, look for the row of sunflowers growing next to the ditch in front." Her aunt winked. "And *gut* luck."

"*Danke.*" Jane chuckled and set off.

She set off toward Levy's house, looking around with interest at her new community. The small town had large homes and neat gardens. Fireflies began flickering over the lawns and fields. Some children played in the spacious front yard of a nearby house; their shrieks and laughter drifted over the road. There seemed to be far fewer *Englischers* living here in Grand Creek than in her hometown in Ohio.

Just ahead, two young women about her age and wearing *kapps* walked toward her. They paused as Jane passed by. "*Gut'n owed!*" one of them said. "Are you visiting here?"

Jane stopped. "*Ja.* I'm Jane Troyer. I just arrived to stay with my aunt and uncle, Peter and Catherine Troyer."

"*Welkom.* I'm Sarah. This is Rhoda…"

Jane chatted with the women for a few minutes. Sarah invited Jane to the same barbecue her uncle had mentioned earlier.

She thanked her for the invitation, then headed on toward Levy's house. She felt the warmth of acceptance and had a feeling it would be no trouble fitting into her new home. Despite the loneliness she sometimes felt as one by one her friends got married and started families, there was a certain excitement about being in a new place and meeting new people.

And she would no longer have to see Isaac, giddy about his new bride. She wouldn't have to witness Hannah's excitement at her first pregnancy. She would no longer have to pretend to be indifferent.

Yes, a whole new community full of new people was just what she needed.

The glow of the kerosene lamp lit the living room as Mercy cried in Levy's arms. He paced back and forth, trying to calm the infant. She'd woken up the moment he'd stepped into the house. Why? What was he doing wrong?

When he heard a knock at the door, he sighed with relief.

Jane stood on his porch, her glasses reflecting the lamplight from within. "Isn't this where I left you?" she joked.

He thrust a hand through his hair and gently bounced the baby. He spoke without greeting. "I've fed her, diapered her. I don't know why she won't stop crying."

"Sounds like she's overly tired. Here, let me take her."

Glad for the break, Levy handed over the infant and stepped away from the door, inviting her inside.

"Shhh, shhhh," Jane whispered. She cradled the baby, swaying a bit as she walked. Levy gestured toward a rocking chair, and she sank down and rocked, cuddling the infant against her chest and murmuring soothing nonsense.

Within moments, Mercy's crying stopped and her little face relaxed.

Levy dropped into a chair opposite. He felt exhausted. "How can you do that?"

"As I said, it's my gift. Enough said." Her voice was clipped.

Levy noticed her curtness, but was too tired to analyze it. "Then I think I've discovered my anti-gift. With me, she won't calm down at all. I can't thank you enough for agreeing to care for her."

Jane set the rocking chair in motion again. "Is there no other woman who can take this baby? It's not going to be easy for a single man to care for her, especially since, as you've said, you have to run your business."

"I'm discovering that. You arrived just as I was going to look for someone else to care for Mercy. That makes you an answer to prayer."

"I've been told I'm good at being *useful*." He thought he saw her eyes tear up, but wasn't sure since she ducked her head to look at the baby. "She's starting to fall asleep, see?"

Levy leaned back in his chair. "It seems like I've been walking her for hours. That's an exaggeration, but not by much. What hours can you work? I'm warning you, I may overwork you."

"My schedule is open. I can work whenever you need me. Within reason," she added.

"What time tomorrow do you want to start?"

"I can be here by eight in the morning. Would that be all right?"

"I hate to ask, but could you make it closer to seven? The days have been very hot lately and I'm trying to get work done outside before the sun is high."

"*Ja*, I can do that."

He nodded, filled with gratitude at this strange woman who had saved him. "Now here's an important question. Can you work Saturdays?"

"I suppose so. But why Saturdays?"

"Because if you remember, I have a booth at the farmer's market. I spend most of my week gearing up for it. Many *Englischers* come to buy produce, so I'll be busy, from dawn until dusk. That's probably when I'll need you the most."

"I'll have to ask my aunt and uncle. Forgive me, Levy, but would it be easier…" She trailed off and didn't finish.

"Let me guess. You were going to ask why I don't give Mercy to another family to raise."

"Well...*ja*."

"*Ja* sure, it would be easier. That's what the bishop wants me to do. But I won't. Not yet. Not until I know whether or not my sister..." He didn't finish his words, unwilling to reveal the deep emotion behind his determination to keep the baby. "If my sister ever comes home, I want her to see I've risen to the challenge of caring for her child."

He was relieved when Jane didn't pursue the matter further. His reasons were his own, and whatever difficult path he had set himself, he was trying to follow it.

"Well, I'll help however I can." Jane shifted the sleeping baby from the crook of her arm to over her shoulder. The infant gave a small sigh and didn't wake. "I think I'll enjoy caring for her."

"I'm grateful." He saw beyond the plain features and thick glasses of this young woman, and noticed instead her sweet expression as she held the baby.

"Well." She rose from the rocking chair. "Where does the *boppli* sleep? I'll put her down."

"In here." Levy picked up the oil lamp and led the way to a bedroom off the kitchen. "This is my room, and it's easiest to have her with me for now."

Late-evening shadows had darkened the room, but he put the lamp on the dresser near the crib so she had light. Jane leaned over and placed the slumbering infant on the mat. She covered her with a light blanket, then tiptoed out of the room.

Levy heaved a sigh as he replaced the lamp on the table. "Ah, *danke*. She's been fussy all day, and I still have barn chores to do."

"Hopefully she'll sleep through the night, so doing chores shouldn't be a problem. I expect she's still getting used to the changes around her. Babies are creatures of habit, so the more she can stay on a regular schedule, the calmer she'll be." Jane walked toward the front door, then turned back to him. "I'll be back tomorrow morning at seven. You can show me where everything is—her formula, diapers and such."

"*Ja*, that's fine. And Jane, *danke*. I had no idea I was so bad with babies."

"Do you still want lessons? Baby lessons?"

"*Ja*. I don't have a choice."

"Then we'll start tomorrow. Don't worry, Levy. If you're determined to raise the baby, you'll learn fast. *Gude nacht*." She smiled and walked out the door.

Levy watched the tall, slender figure walk down the darkening street. Jane wasn't pretty in the conventional sense, but she had a remarkably calming quality about her. Not just with Mercy, but somehow he felt more composed in her presence.

He shook his head. There was more to Jane than met the eye, that was for sure. He was just very grateful she'd agreed to care for Mercy.

Jane retraced her path down the quiet road toward her aunt and uncle's house. No streetlights or car headlights broke the darkness, but fireflies twinkled over the fields and warm lamplight shone from windows.

So she had a job now, a job where she could be *useful*. Levy needed help, no question. In addition to caring for little Mercy, she was glad Levy wanted some parenting lessons. All in all, it had been an eventful day, and she realized how tired she was.

But being *useful* kept darker thoughts at bay. She tried not to think of the cozy home she'd left behind, with her mother and father, her younger sisters, her brothers. Her married older sister was expecting a baby. And Jane would miss all that.

When her *mamm* half-jokingly offered to arrange a marriage for her, Jane knew it was time to leave. She wasn't sure an arranged marriage was the right thing for her, at least not right now.

Here in this new community, she wouldn't linger over the past. She would look only at the present—her new job, becoming acquainted with people her age, spending some time with her aunt and uncle. Yes, she had a lot on her plate, and she was grateful for it.

Maybe caring for little Mercy full-time would fill the ache that came from knowing she was unlikely ever to have a baby of her own.

Chapter Three

Early the next morning, Jane walked toward Levy's home. Mist burned off from across the fields, and the sun shone through it in streaming bars of light. The air was cool and fresh. She walked up to the house and knocked on the front door.

"Come in!" he called.

Morning sunshine poured through the windows as she walked in, lighting a room that was comfortable but not clean. Dusting and sweeping, apparently, had gone by the wayside with little Mercy's arrival.

"In here!" called Levy.

Jane dropped the bag she'd carried onto the floor and followed his voice into the bedroom off the kitchen. Levy was changing the baby's diaper.

"At least she's not crying," observed Jane, leaning against the doorframe.

"*Ja*, something of a marvel. All right, *geliebte*, almost finished…"

"You're actually not bad at that." Jane watched as he

tucked the cloth diaper neatly into a diaper cover around the baby's bottom and fastened the straps.

"Amazing what I've learned since Mercy arrived," he admitted. He slipped a flannel dress over the baby's head and pushed her little arms into the correct holes.

"Where did you get the diapers and baby clothes?"

"People in the church donated them. I had to buy the bottles and formula, though." He lifted the baby up.

"Here, I'll take her," Jane said.

Levy placed the baby into Jane's arms, and her heart melted a bit at the sweet-smelling little bundle. "Goodness, she's such a precious baby."

"*Ja.* When she's not crying, that is." He ran a hand through his hair. "She's just a whole lot more work than I ever anticipated."

"Well, it doesn't sound like you had any warning."

"That's an understatement. Let me show you around, so you know where to find things."

Jane trailed behind as he showed her where the baby's diapers, formula, bottles, clothing and other things were located. She was pleased to see the bouncy seat on the table, which would allow the infant to be present during meals or other kitchen activities.

"I know it's awkward to be in someone else's home," he concluded, "especially since you're just settling in with your aunt and uncle."

"*Ja*, I was going to ask about that. Do you mind if I go back and forth between here and there?"

"*Nein*, of course not. I trust you to do whatever you need to do with Mercy." He glanced at a clock over the kitchen sink. "But I need to get to work. Will you be okay on your own?"

Jane chuckled. "Probably better than *you* are on your own."

His eyes crinkled with amusement. "Help yourself to anything in the kitchen, and feel free to explore the house and property." He picked up his hat, plopped it on his head and strode out the door.

Jane watched as he seized several garden tools and walked toward fields planted deep with corn and other vegetables. Beyond the barn she saw fenced pastures where three cows and their calves grazed. A rooster crowed from a coop near the barn, and she saw a tangle of fencing that could only be a pigpen. In all ways, Levy's property was a typical Amish small farm.

She looked down at Mercy, who gazed back with unfocused eyes. Jane dropped a kiss on the baby's nose. "It's just you and me, little one. What shall we do first?"

She began by taking Levy up on his offer and exploring the house. It was smaller than most Amish homes, just two dusty, unused bedrooms upstairs, a cellar below, and the rest of the living quarters on the first floor, including the master bedroom he shared with the infant. A treadle sewing machine occupied one corner of the living room. A small room off the living room turned out to be an office. From the ledgers and notepads, she concluded it's where he did his accounting work.

Mercy looked ready to fall asleep, so Jane sat in a rocking chair until the baby drifted off. She noticed the film of dust on the furniture, the unswept floors, the clutter of unwashed dishes in the kitchen sink. Levy needed more than a nanny for this motherless infant—he needed a housekeeper. She wondered why he wasn't married. Unlike her, he was an attractive person. Surely some woman would notice that?

When Mercy had fallen asleep, Jane laid the baby in her crib, then tackled the house. She explored the basement and found shelves of canned food and jars of dried beans, as well as hundreds of empty canning jars. Selecting some split peas and a jar of canned ham, she went upstairs and started making some split-pea soup for lunch. She washed the piles of dishes. She dusted and swept the entire downstairs.

Mercy awoke with a wail, so Jane changed her diaper and sat down in the rocking chair to feed her a bottle. It was then that Levy returned.

"Soup!" He sniffed the air. "I didn't expect you to cook, Jane, but it sure smells good."

"What would you normally eat midday?"

"Just a sandwich or two." He ladled the steaming soup into a bowl. "And you did the dishes!"

"This house needs a woman's touch." Jane lifted the bouncy seat on the table and laid Mercy in it. "There, *liebling*, now you can watch as we eat."

"Was she good this morning?"

"Like gold. She's such a sweet baby."

Levy closed his eyes for a silent prayer, then swallowed a spoonful. "It was *Gott*'s will you got stranded at that train station. Already I don't know what I'd do without you."

For just a moment, Jane's heart gave a thump. Whatever happened, she wouldn't let herself become attracted to Levy. She wouldn't. "I'm grateful for the job." Her remark was deliberate, to remind Levy she worked for him and nothing else.

"Mercy seems happy too." He toyed with the baby's feet, encased in thin flannel socks. "Maybe she knows she's no longer subject to a fumbling bachelor's care. How late can you work?" he added.

"What time do you normally finish working outside?"

"Dinnertime, though I often do an hour or two of accounting afterward."

"Maybe I should put it this way—what time do you feel up to taking over Mercy's care?"

He rubbed his chin, a look of frustration darkening his blue eyes. "To be honest, I don't feel up to it at all, but I know that's not a realistic attitude. I can't keep you here around the clock."

"I wasn't joking about offering baby lessons, if you really want them."

"I don't have a choice at this point, especially since I plan to keep her."

"But for the time being, how about I stay until after dinner? I don't mind cooking."

"*Danke*. Since you didn't sign up for cooking meals, I can pay you a bit extra."

"Can you afford it?" She clapped a hand over her mouth. "That was rude. I'm sorry. Your finances are none of my business."

He laughed. "Don't worry, I'll manage."

"Then *ja, danke*. And in addition to cooking, I can do housekeeping—laundry and dishes and tidying up."

"I think we'll get along together well. I'm grateful, Jane."

"Forget the gratitude and just show me where you keep your washing machine. I'll do a load of laundry this afternoon."

The swing-handled nonelectric washing machine was stored in a shed off the back porch. After Levy went back to work, Jane fed Mercy, changed her diaper then strapped the baby back in her bouncy seat on the porch. Jane sang as she washed a load of diapers, more for Mercy's sake than her own. Then she washed some of Levy's clothes and hung them to dry on the clothesline.

"Come on, *liebling*, let's go look at your uncle's garden and see what we can find to make dinner." She lifted the baby over her shoulder, picked up a large basket and walked out to the gated space filled with vegetables.

However messy Levy's house had been, his garden was a thing of beauty, tidy and weeded. Jane spied the prolific zucchini and decided to make zucchini casserole for dinner. She filled her basket with four of the green squashes, then dug up a couple of onions and some garlic. Back in the house, she had the casserole assembled within a few minutes and popped it into the oven to bake.

Mercy started to fuss, so Jane eased the baby onto her shoulder and sat down in the rocking chair, humming lullabies and rocking the child. The afternoon was warm and Jane was tired. Her humming grew slower and softer.

Next thing she knew, she blinked her eyes open to see Levy standing nearby.

"Oh." She felt her face grow warm. "I must have fallen asleep."

"Don't worry about it."

"The casserole…!" The infant gave a small start at Jane's small cry of alarm but didn't wake up.

"It's out of the oven and on the warming rack."

She settled back into the chair and shook her head. "I can't imagine why I did that, falling asleep on the job, I'm so sorry…"

"Jane, I can see how much work you've done this afternoon. Don't apologize." He grinned. "It was actually rather a sweet sight, coming in to find you both asleep."

Her face flushed warmer. "*Ja*, well, I'll just go put Mercy in her crib."

She stood up and kept the infant cradled on her shoulder, but the moment she stepped foot in the kitchen, she stopped in her tracks. "What on earth…"

"I'm not a total klutz in the kitchen." Levy chuckled.

The table was neatly set for two, and the casserole was covered and on the stove's warming rack.

"You didn't have to do this…" she began.

"Why not? Stop feeling guilty, Jane. It didn't take me long."

She nodded and disappeared into the bedroom to lay Mercy in her crib. She took a few deep breaths before leaving the room. Falling asleep her first day on the job—how embarrassing.

When she reemerged, Levy dished up the food and filled the plates. Jane bowed her head for grace, then reached for her fork. "Your garden is beautiful. After seeing the state of your house, I didn't expect it to be so nice."

"*Ja*, I'm more of an outdoorsman than an indoor one. I can weed all day, but I don't see anything that needs doing inside."

"Which is why everything was so thick with dust." Jane swallowed a bite. "But it will be easier to keep up now that I cleaned everything."

"Oh, did you clean everything?"

She chuckled. "Typical man who doesn't see dust bunnies until they're big enough to bite. Don't worry, I took care of them."

"And you did laundry too. And made lunch and dinner. And took care of Mercy."

"And you worked in the fields all day. We both have our jobs, then."

"Still, you seem like a very organized person."

Jane's smile faded. "I've been told I'm a very *useful* person."

"Is that such a bad thing?"

"*Nein… Nein*, I guess not." *Unless it came from the man she loved.* She shoved the thought of Isaac behind her. "So I guess I'll accept being useful."

"Being useful has its advantages."

"And it's what I'm good at. I try not to be bitter about it." She hadn't meant to be so open with Levy.

He raised his eyebrows. "Bitter? Why would you be bitter about something like that?"

"It's nothing."

"Does this reference have to do with your mysterious past that we talked about yesterday on the way home from the train station?"

"Maybe." She rose, trying not to feel flustered. "Are you finished? I'll wash up before I head home."

"You're changing the subject, but that's okay. I'll take advantage of the baby sleeping and start my accounting work."

As Jane washed and rinsed bowls and cutlery, she found herself grateful for Levy's restraint. He clearly wanted to know about her past, but didn't probe. Levy was the last person she wanted to learn about her background.

With just two people to feed, dishes took only a few minutes. Jane peeked in at the baby and found her still sleeping. She frowned and wondered if such solid napping this late in the afternoon meant Levy might be in for a long night with a wide-awake infant. She'd have to work harder to get little Mercy on a better sleep schedule.

"I'll head home now," she announced to Levy. Late-evening sunshine poured into his office window.

He looked up from a scattering of papers, pen in hand. "*Vielen Dank* for everything you did today, Jane."

"I'll be here around seven o'clock tomorrow morning. But since tomorrow is Friday, I should let you know I was invited to attend a barbeque tomorrow evening. It would be a good chance for me to get to know some of the young people around here."

He frowned. "Fridays are busy for me, since that's the day I prepare for the farmer's market."

"Well, I'll be here all day. I'll just be leaving a bit early, is all."

He looked doubtful. "All right, then. Good night."

Why would Levy seem unhappy that she had a social event planned? Jane wondered at his odd reaction. She walked back to her aunt and uncle's house and found them relaxing with hot cocoa and the *Budget* newspapers on the front porch.

"How did your first full day of work go?" asked Catherine.

"Fine." Jane plopped down in a spare rocking chair and sighed. "And I got a raise, so to speak. Levy's house was a mess, so he offered me extra pay to add cooking and housekeeping duties in addition to watching the baby."

Catherine chuckled. "He's had his hands full, no doubt."

"Why isn't anyone else helping him?"

"I think it just hadn't gotten to that point yet," her aunt replied. "He was obviously going to need help the moment Eliza sent the baby to him, but I think he had a crazy idea he could do it all himself. Now he's finding he can't, and that's just when you arrived."

"I think Levy doesn't believe me when I say she's easy to care for, though my arms got a little tired with carrying her so much."

"Would you like a baby sling?" Catherine asked. "I still have one tucked away."

"*Ja*, I'd forgotten about those! That would be wonderful."

Catherine disappeared for a few minutes, then came back out to the porch carrying a soft cotton garment. "You remember how to wear this, right?"

"I think so." Jane slipped the sling over her shoulder and mimed cradling an infant in it. "I'm surprised you still have this."

"It's been a while since I used it, but with three grandchildren so far, I still use it occasionally. Remember, until she's old enough to sit up, you carry the baby either like this, or like this." Catherine demonstrated infant positions.

Jane nodded and copied her actions. "This will help a lot, since it means I can carry Mercy while working around the house. Levy did tell me I was free to bring her here, or go anywhere I want with her too."

"Then that sling will be useful everywhere."

Jane winced at the term *useful* but didn't say anything. Instead, she looked over the peaceful lawn illuminated by late-evening sun and sighed. Overall she was glad to be here in Grand Creek. But was this the best place for her? Only time would tell.

When she arrived at Levy's the next morning, she found him outside near the barn constructing something. Mercy was strapped into her bouncy seat nearby.

"*Guder mariye.*" Without asking, Jane removed the infant from the seat and lifted her into her arms.

"*Guder mariye.*" Levy stopped working and fished out a red bandanna to wipe a trickle of sweat from beneath his straw hat. "*Ach*, it's going to be a hot day. Already the sun is warm."

"What are you building?"

"Remember those boxes I picked up at the train station? It's a new booth for the farmer's market." He pocketed the bandanna. "Just confirming, you said you can work on Saturdays, *ja*?"

His eyes had dark circles around them, and Jane wondered how many times he'd gotten up with the baby. But she frowned. Just how much time was this job going to entail? Would she ever have a day off?

"I can work Saturday," she assured him. "And perhaps in exchange I can take a day off during the week." She paused as he looked unhappy. "Levy, I can't work here every day, all day. I have a life too."

"*Ja*, I know." The strain increased on his face. "Though I work every day, and I don't know what I'll do without you."

"You may have to hire someone else for the days I take off."

"Maybe." He didn't look happy as he glanced upward at his construction project. "This is almost finished. I'll spend the rest of the day picking and crating up the produce I'll sell tomorrow."

"What will you sell?"

"Corn, onions, garlic, some late strawberries, raspberries—lots of raspberries, they're peaking now—tomatoes, lettuce, spinach…" he continued, ticking down the list of foods.

"Definitely sounds like you have a full day ahead of you." Jane glanced at the baby. "Will it be convenient for me to leave by six o'clock tonight so I can make it to the barbecue?"

He shoved a crate. "Why are you going to that?"

She arched her eyebrows at the question. "That's kind of rude. Why shouldn't I go? I think it's important to meet others in the community."

He frowned. "Seems a very frivolous thing to do."

"Fortunately, it's not your place to dictate what I can and cannot do." Jane's voice was tart.

He scrubbed a hand over his face, but remained silent.

Jane knew he was tired. "I can work tomorrow, don't worry."

Levy just nodded and went back to his work.

She didn't see him until lunchtime. She caught glimpses of him outside, picking corn or gathering tomatoes or plucking raspberries.

"Do you need help?" she asked, as he wolfed down the grilled cheese sandwiches she'd made for lunch. "It's an awful lot of work for one man to do alone."

"You're helping enough, trust me." He wiped his mouth and gulped the milk from his glass. He glanced at the clock. "Back to work."

It was her first glimpse into the heavy schedule Levy set himself. All day long, he picked fruits and vegetables and hauled them back to the cool barn. The delicate raspberries he brought into the house, and Jane put them down in the basement. Levy didn't complain about the workload, but Jane could tell he was stressed.

She did a load of laundry, gave the house a quick

dusting and sweeping, made a hearty dinner, washed the dishes and made sure Mercy was bathed and diapered.

"Don't forget," she reminded him toward evening. "I'll be leaving in a few minutes."

"Oh that's right." He made a face of dismay. "That means I'm back to taking care of the baby."

"I know you're busy, but ultimately she's your responsibility, not mine." Jane tried not to let her temper rise. "I can't work all the time."

"Well, *I* work all the time."

She lifted her chin. The martyr act wouldn't work on her. "That's your choice. Now, what time do you need me here tomorrow?"

"Early, if you can. The farmer's market opens by nine o'clock, so I plan to leave here by seven at the latest. You'll have to pack a diaper bag for her…"

"Diaper bag?" Jane raised her eyebrows. "You mean I'll be working the market with you? I thought I'd just stay home with the baby. Wouldn't that be easier?"

"Surprisingly, no. A second pair of hands is best, if for no other reason than the occasional break." He offered a thin smile.

Quickly, she adjusted her thinking. Working at a farmer's market actually sounded like fun. "I'll be here by six thirty then. That way I can handle the baby while you pack the wagon."

His nod was curt. "*Danke.*"

"Good night, Levy." She handed him Mercy.

Her annoyance faded as she walked back toward her aunt and uncle's. His apparent objections to her attending the barbecue seemed deeper than mere inconvenience regarding childcare or a busy schedule. Was there a problem with the *youngies* in town? Instinct told her it was something more. She wondered if she'd ever learn what it was.

As Levy watched Jane walk away, he couldn't shake the eerie feeling he was watching his sister walk away to attend a *youngie* event. Eliza had always been keen to get away from him, from her home, from her responsibilities. For a fraction of an instant, he saw his sister's retreating figure instead of Jane's.

Then he shook his head and snapped out of it. It was unfair to project his worries over Eliza's fate on the woman who had kindly taken on the chore of caring for her baby. Jane was nothing like his sister. She was steady, levelheaded and incredibly efficient.

For once, Mercy lay quiet in his arms. He looked down at her tiny face, trying to see his sister in her features, wondering where Eliza was and if she missed her baby.

Then he looked up, but Jane had already disappeared down the road. He was glad she was coming to the farmer's market with him tomorrow—for deeper reasons than merely caring for the baby.

He didn't want to examine those deeper reasons. Not yet.

Chapter Four

That evening, as Jane got ready for the barbecue, she tried not to be annoyed at Levy. He was stressed, no question. Most Amish men worked hard, but it seemed to her Levy worked *too* hard. It was tough enough to operate a small farm solo. Throw in the complication of an abandoned baby, and it was a recipe for strain and pressure.

Her thoughts went to the barbecue and all the people she would meet.

"Are you nervous?" Catherine asked.

"*Ja*, maybe." Jane washed her face and tidied her hair at the kitchen sink as her aunt lingered nearby. "Back home, I knew everyone. Here I don't. It's just something I have to face, getting used to a new crowd."

"They're a nice group." Catherine handed Jane her *kapp*. "I'm sure you'll have fun."

"Except I'll feel guilty all evening, leaving Levy in charge of Mercy. He wasn't happy about it." Jane pinned on her *kapp* and slipped a clean apron over her dress.

"He's going to have to get used to caring for her, that's all there is to it." Her aunt gave her directions to the host farm. "Have fun at the barbecue, *lieb*."

"*Danke*." Jane kissed her aunt's cheek and set off down the road.

The farm hosting the barbecue was a mile away. Catherine had told her the Yoder family, with four teenagers still at home, enjoyed hosting *youngie* events. Already dozens of people were gathered in the front yard under the shade trees. Jane thought she was looking forward to the event, but now that it was at hand, she wondered if she would fit in. It was one thing to grow up in a community and know everyone since birth. But she knew no one here. She shoved her glasses higher on her nose, took a deep breath and walked on.

Sarah, the young woman she'd met earlier, spied her right away. "You came!"

"*Ja*, thank you for letting me know about it." Jane glanced at the young people milling about, chattering, laughing, roasting hot dogs over a pit fire.

"I'll introduce you around, if you like," offered Sarah.

"I'll never remember everyone's names," warned Jane. "But please introduce me."

What should have been a fun evening with new friends was anything but. Jane felt shy and awkward despite the support of Sarah and Rhoda, who took her under their wing.

"I feel like I'm sixteen instead of twenty-three," she groused to Sarah as she sprawled on the lawn with her new friends, learning each of their stories. "Will I ever grow out of being awkward, do you suppose?"

"I'm sure it's just because you're in a new place," soothed Rhoda. "You'll fit in just fine when you have a chance to know more people. That's why I think you should keep coming to singings and other *youngie* events. How else will you get to know anyone?"

"*Ja*, true…" Jane trailed off, thinking about Levy's awkwardness while being in sole charge of the baby.

"Besides, we're glad you've come." Sarah spoke with such simple sincerity that Jane's eyes felt hot. She loved the Amish sense of community.

"And it seems it was *Gott*'s will to find a job the moment I arrived too," she replied. "Levy Struder—do you know him?—he's taking care of his sister's child. He hired me as the baby's nanny."

"Oh, Levy, he's a *gut* man," said Sarah.

"He seems a little old to be single. Why isn't he married?" Jane asked, trying to keep her question casual.

"It all goes back to his sister," Sarah answered, nibbling a cookie. "He practically raised her after their parents died, and when she left for her *Rumspringa* and didn't come back, he took it very hard. I think he's afraid he'll mess up with everyone—a wife, his own children—so he never sought out the responsibility of a family. Which is pretty ironic, since he loves kids."

"Yet he thinks he can raise little Mercy on his own," observed Jane. "He refuses to give her to another family to raise."

"He's really eaten up by guilt over his sister," said

Sarah. "He can't bear the thought of giving up his sister's baby."

"Did she…ah, was she not married?" asked Jane.

"I don't know." Rhoda looked troubled. "No one knows for sure, but why else would she give up her baby if she had a husband?"

"Well, I'll do the best I can for the *boppli*, but I hope Levy remembers I'm just the nanny, not the baby's mother."

"What do you mean?"

"He's very busy running his business. Two businesses, actually. Plus the baby isn't sleeping through the night. I could literally have the care of her for twenty-four hours a day, seven days a week, and I don't think it would be enough time for him. Each evening when I go home, I feel guilty for leaving Mercy to Levy. I think he's scared to be in sole charge of her."

"Did you have a hard time getting away to come to the barbecue tonight?" asked Rhoda.

"*Ja*. I mean, he didn't argue with me, but he got an odd look on his face." Jane mimicked Levy's expression so accurately the other girls laughed.

"I hope you can keep coming to the *youngie* events." Sarah looked around at the chattering groups of young people lit up by the flickering flames of the pit fire. "We have activities just about every week during the summer. A lot of people knew someone was coming to stay with your aunt and uncle, and we were anxious to get to know you."

She felt a quiver of unease. It seemed her adolescent awkwardness had never left her. She'd never really cultivated the social graces, and now she had to plunge outside her comfort zone. Had she made a mistake to leave home where she knew everyone, to immerse herself with strangers?

Yet Rhoda was right. If she didn't keep coming to these events, how else would she get to know anyone?

"It's late." Rhoda climbed to her feet and dusted off her dress. "It's been so hot lately, so we work outside in the garden in the early morning. I'd best get home."

Others were departing as well, carrying empty food containers and walking through the darkness toward their homes. Jane walked alone—it was something she was used to—and headed for her aunt and uncle's house.

In a moment of insight, she realized why she'd cultivated being *useful*. It covered for her plain looks, her awkward social skills. Everyone needed a *useful* woman.

She had been useful back home in Jasper. She would be useful here in Grand Creek, too.

She had cause to regret her decision to be useful by the next morning.

She arrived at Levy's to find the baby wailing in her bouncy seat on the porch. Levy was loading boxes and baskets of produce into the wagon, which was already hitched to the horse.

"She's all yours," he snapped, his face tense. "I've got a lot to do before we leave."

Jane didn't say a word. Levy's anxiety had communicated itself to little Mercy, and the baby cried louder.

She picked up the infant and cradled her in her arms. "I'm here, hush now, hush…"

It took some time for the infant to calm down, and even then she was edgy and cranky. Jane stayed out of Levy's way while he dashed around. Instead, she concentrated on packing what she needed for the baby: a diaper bag with bottles of formula, several changes of clothing and diapers, a light blanket, the sling, the padded basket used as a cradle and the bouncy seat. For herself and Levy, she packed a large lunch since she suspected he'd forgotten about food for himself.

Levy poked his head through the kitchen door. "Can you be ready in five minutes?"

"I'll be ready." Slipping the baby into the sling, Jane picked up the diaper bag and a food hamper and walked outside.

The wagon was loaded to capacity with the shelving, displays, chairs, tools, a scale and all the other accoutrements of a farmer's market booth. Boxes and crates and baskets of produce bulged at the corners. He'd even stuffed two bales of straw into the side. Jane managed to wedge the food hamper and diaper bag in a tight corner.

"Here, I'll hold the baby while you climb up." Levy appeared from the barn, mopped his brow with a bandanna and took the baby while Jane scrambled onto the wagon seat. She leaned down and took Mercy and settled the baby back into the sling while Levy stepped up, took the reins and started the horse down the road.

"Sorry I was so busy. I overslept," he apologized.

"Let me guess—Mercy was up during the night?"

"*Ja*. I meant to get up much earlier, I fell back asleep

after feeding her, and the next thing I knew the sun was already up when I opened my eyes. I dashed around getting all the chores done, but I'm afraid I didn't have much time to devote to the baby, except for feeding and diapering her."

"Well, don't worry about her for now. I'll take care of her." She thought about her conversation with Sarah and Rhoda last night at the barbecue, about Levy's determination to keep the baby. Personally she thought the bishop was right and Levy should give Mercy to another family to raise. It was clearly too much for him to run his business and care for such a tiny infant.

But he'd already told her he didn't want to give Mercy up without knowing if his sister would return. Plus he was a stubborn man. She looked down at the baby in the sling. The child's eyes were heavy. After the anxious atmosphere of the morning, she seemed ready to sleep. Jane chose not to voice her doubts about Levy's decision to keep Mercy. "I'm grateful for the work, and I enjoy caring for the *boppli*, however long the arrangement lasts."

"Right now I'm too busy to think long-term. All I know is…" His voice trailed off.

Jane glanced at him, then looked out at the scenery going by. She promised herself not to bring up his sister anymore. The subject was clearly too personal, too raw for him. He wouldn't give up Mercy because doing so would be giving up on Mercy's mother, his sister. That much was obvious.

"I'll do my best to ease your burden," she said instead. "I like caring for babies."

"*Danke.*"

She lapsed into silence as Mercy fell asleep. Feeling the precious weight against her chest, her feelings toward the baby—already warm—altered. There were worse jobs than to act as a surrogate mother to this baby.

The farmer's market was held in a shady park that took up nearly one entire city block in an otherwise quiet residential neighborhood. A section was fenced off for Amish horses and buggies, and the parking lot was for vendors only.

"Do customers have to park on the streets?" inquired Jane, looking around.

"*Ja.* The whole farmer's market takes on an air of a festival every weekend. They even arrange for some children's entertainment, clown shows and such." Levy guided the horse through the parking area. "It's a whole lot more popular than the size of the town suggests. I'm fortunate it's so close by."

A clatter of other wagons crowded the streets, and Amish families started setting up their own stalls and booths. Levy called out to a number of them.

"*Hei*, what a lot of vendors!" Jane exclaimed. The place was packed.

"Ja. You won't believe the crowds that will come later," Levy answered.

He pulled up by an empty space and climbed down from the wagon, then raised his arms for Mercy. Jane handed him the sleeping infant, then climbed down from the wagon and took the baby again. "What do you want me to do?"

"I have to figure out how to set up this new booth.

While I work on that, can you unload boxes of produce? Or would that be too much while you're holding
the baby?" He seemed to be over his earlier dark mood.

He grinned at her, which made Jane catch her breath.
Levy's rare smiles transformed him from a rather grim
man to an unnervingly handsome one. His dark blue
eyes glinted in the dappled sunshine. To hide her reaction, she concentrated on slipping Mercy into the
padded basket Levy used as a makeshift cradle without waking her. "*Nein*, unloading boxes shouldn't be a
problem. I'll just make sure she's safe in the shade by
that tree."

With Mercy sleeping in the basket, she deposited the
diaper bag and food hamper nearby, then began unloading crates of produce while Levy figured out how to
assemble his new booth.

The park was busy with vendors setting up. The
scope of the market amazed her. Dozens of booths were
being assembled. Not all were run by Amish families.
She saw many *Englisch* farmers as well, setting out
crates of tomatoes, corn, peppers and other vegetables
and fruits. A few early shoppers wandered around, but
most sellers weren't quite ready to open for business yet.
She received friendly nods and greetings from neigh-
boring sellers.

"Here, can you hold this?" asked Levy. He indicated
a pole. "I need to fasten these two pieces together. *Ja*,
just like that."

Jane helped balance various components while the
booth took shape under Levy's hands.

Finally he stepped back. "What do you think?"

"It looks *gut!*" she replied. "I don't know what your previous booth looked like, but this seems spacious and welcoming."

"*Danke.*" He began setting out baskets of tomatoes, propped up at an inviting angle on a display rack. "I think it will work out well."

Jane began hauling boxes of produce over, but then Mercy woke up, so instead she grabbed one of the two folding chairs Levy had brought and set it next to the nearby tree. She found a bottle of formula in the diaper bag and settled in to feed the *boppli*.

"What's that?" Levy pointed to the hamper next to the diaper bag.

"Lunch. And breakfast, for that matter."

"*Gut!* I completely forgot." He smiled at a family who wandered by and stopped to examine the produce for sale.

"Does this farmer's market have an official opening time?" Jane settled the baby more comfortably in the crook of her arm.

Levy waited until the potential customers moved on, then he dove into the food hamper, pulled out some biscuits and began eating. "I was so busy this morning I didn't have time for breakfast. As for when it opens—it's somewhat informal, though vendors are asked to finish unloading and move their cars and wagons by 9:00 a.m. We have to stay until five o'clock, though, by the rules."

"Rules? Is it that structured?"

"*Ja.* We sign an agreement. I can understand why they have these rules, otherwise a vendor might depart early and leave a big gaping hole where his booth was. Good morning!" he added to a young mother with two children in tow.

Once Mercy was fed, Jane slipped the infant into the sling and helped Levy stock the booth, spreading out the fresh fruits and vegetables in beautiful eye-catching displays.

"Having you here is sure useful," he murmured as the crowds grew thick. "It's nice to have another pair of hands to help out."

She flushed with pleasure, even at the term *useful*. "I'm still learning," she warned him. "I've never worked with customers before."

"Then you're a natural. Keep it up."

His praise was all she needed to redouble her efforts. Watching Levy sell his farm produce was a revelation to Jane. His booth was thronged almost from the beginning, and he easily outsold nearly every other vendor in the park. It was easy to see why. Unlike most Amish men, he was not reserved, but animated. He joked, he chatted, he bantered. She estimated half his customers were regulars, but several times she noticed people stopped at the booth because they wondered why it was so crowded.

And she knew it would have been extraordinarily difficult for him to function this way without someone watching Mercy.

Jane stayed busy too. When Mercy was quiet—either tucked in her sling or resting in the cradle basket—she helped weigh and bag produce, make change and restock the crates and baskets with fresh food. But she lacked Levy's easy way with strangers, especially *Englischers*.

During a rare quiet moment, she collapsed on the chair. "How do you do it?" She gulped water from a jar. "You behave like you've had classes in salesmanship."

"In a way I have." He bit into a sandwich. "When I first started selling here, my booth was right next to an older man—an *Englischer*—who was retiring and moving to Florida. His name was Robert and he was wonderful with customers. He wasn't pushy, he was friendly. I watched him and learned. It's a little difficult for me—I'm not a salesman by nature—but this is how I make my living, and if I'm going to sell produce, I have to sell it in the very best way possible. It puts me way outside my comfort zone, for sure and certain. I'm grateful to *Gott* for putting my booth next to Robert's. If I'd been anywhere else, I never would have watched him in action and seen how well he did."

"Did he know you were watching him?"

"Of course. In fact, he spent the whole summer coaching me. He gave me pointers and tips for improving my sales. I'd never done anything like this before, so it was a steep learning curve. But I find it tiring. By the end of the day, I'm wiped out and need a whole week to recover."

"I can understand that." The crowds were hard for Jane to get used to as well. "I'm surprised this little town has so many people coming to its farmer's market."

"They advertise farther away, in many communities around here. I've had people tell me they drive an hour to get here so they can stock up on their week's groceries. The success of this little market far surpasses the boundaries of the town, for sure and certain. The people who run the market know what they're doing."

Their brief respite ended when more people stopped by to browse the produce, and Levy's booth stayed busy until late in the afternoon.

"What did you do with Mercy last week?" she asked at one point, after the baby woke up from a nap and cried until Jane fed her again.

"The teenage *youngie* I hired watched her," he admitted. "I didn't have a choice. You can see how busy I am on market days. They're $3.99 a pound," he told a customer, smiling as he sold the last of his raspberries. "But having you here changes the whole dynamic, even with the *boppli*. I'm not nearly as stressed."

Jane quivered. His gratitude seemed to hold a note of something more, something deeper than just recognition that she was a useful sales associate. Or was she imagining it?

The pressure of customer demands didn't ease until just before the market was due to close. But Levy seemed in no hurry to break down and pack up any remaining inventory. "Always be the last to close," he explained to Jane. "That's another trick of the trade Robert taught me. You'd be surprised how many times people want to make one last purchase before they leave for the day."

This proved true when not one, but *three* late customers cleaned out the rest of Levy's tomatoes, corn and onions. Other booths were in a state of disassembly, but Levy's little store was still open for business.

With the clock edging toward 5:30, a weary Jane laid Mercy in her cradle basket and helped Levy collect what small amount of produce remained unsold.

"I'll go hitch up Maggie and get the wagon," he said.

Left alone, she stacked what she could and repacked their food hamper. After a few minutes, Levy guided his horse and wagon nearby, and they began disassembling the booth components and loading them into the wagon.

Finally they started for home. "That was intense." Jane sighed.

"*Ja.* I think it's more intense because they only hold the farmer's market on Saturdays. So many of their vendors are Amish and we won't work on the Sabbath, and people know that, so everyone crowds in to make their purchases on that one day."

"Do you like selling there?" Jane waved to another departing vendor.

"It's not a question of like, it's a question of practicality. It's convenient." Levy stopped at an intersection, then guided the horse through. "During the summer and early fall, I earn almost my entire year's income from the farmer's market or Community Supported Agriculture subscriptions. That means I have buyers who take excess produce every week."

"And during the rest of the year, you supplement your income with accounting?"

"*Ja.* It gets very busy before tax day, so I do a lot of bookkeeping over the winter. It's been a precarious income, but this is the first year I've done better financially."

"Seeing how hard you work makes me feel guilty for accepting money to nanny the baby." She hugged the quiet baby resting in her arms.

"You work hard too. I think it's *Gott*'s timing. My business started doing well just when I needed to hire a nanny. We roll with the punches in this life, dealing with whatever *Gott* hands us."

"*Ja*, I suppose." She lapsed into silence, idly watching the town pass by. Finally she thought to ask, "I assume you won't need me tomorrow on the Sabbath?"

"Well, I wouldn't *say* that." Levy's mouth curved into a thin smile. "But it's the Sabbath. I can't ask you to work on your day of rest."

"But no rest for the weary *onkel*, eh?"

"Right. I'll cope somehow."

Jane had her private doubts that he would be able to, but she let it go.

He dropped her off directly at her aunt and uncle's house. "*Vielen Dank*, Jane. You were incredibly helpful and useful today." He touched his hat brim, spoke to the horse and drove away.

Jane stared after him. *Useful* again. She blinked back tears and realized she didn't want Levy to appreciate her *useful* qualities, but perhaps something more.

All day long she had worked side by side with Levy. Perhaps it had been her imagination, but she got the impression he was appreciating her for more than her usefulness. Now, it seems, she was wrong.

A small part of her wanted him to appreciate her for more than that.

Chapter Five

Sabbath mornings were different from the rest of the week. Jane looked forward to the church services. It was more than a chance to take a break from the relentless work, to focus on *Gott*, to pray.

It was also a chance for the community to come together, for her to see the friends she'd made and perhaps meet new ones. The thought made Jane clasp and unclasp her hands in her lap. Making new friends was difficult for her.

Wearing clean clothes and a freshly starched *kapp*, she rode with Uncle Peter and Aunt Catherine toward the home of the Millers, who were hosting the week's worship service. Many buggies joined them on the road as they headed out, with occupants waving greetings.

"*Ach*, there's young Lydia Yoder with Jacob. Looks like she's about to have her baby any day now," commented Catherine.

Jane peered around the edge of the buggy and saw a pretty young matron, heavily pregnant. "Is it her first?"

"*Ja*. She's very happy."

"And there's Phillip Herschberger." Uncle Peter waved an arm. "He broke his leg last month. I think he'll be getting the cast off shortly."

"And that's the Stoltzfus family. They own the hardware store near our store."

"I see Moses Bontrager." Uncle Peter nodded toward an incoming buggy. "He's been down with the flu. I'm so glad to see him up and about."

So the comments about friends and neighbors in the community continued all the way to the Sabbath service. The older Miller boys directed buggies and horses, and men unhitched their animals and led them into a spacious shady corral for the day. Uncle Peter swung out of the buggy, handed down Jane and Catherine and unhitched his own horse.

Back in her hometown of Jasper, Jane had loved Church Sundays. People came together for a single purpose—worship—but it was much more. It was a reinforcement of their identity, a chance to visit and strengthen bonds of friends and family and an opportunity to learn who might need help.

And now she had to join a whole new community. Jane resisted the urge to cling like a child to her aunt's skirt and hide from strangers, as she used to do with her mother. She was a grown woman, and grown women weren't supposed to be tongue-tied or self-conscious.

Everywhere she looked, people clustered in groups, chatting in subdued tones. Many women carried covered bowls and platters of food into the Millers' kitchen, even though the service was being held in the large barn, where benches had been set up the day before. Children ran around, their shirts or dresses as colorful as flowers.

There were so many new people to meet, many of whom were her age. Jane's heart should have swelled with the thought of new acquaintances who would not consider her a useful person, but instead a fun, even enjoyable person—but she was fooling herself. With sudden insight, she realized one of the reasons she made herself useful was that she knew she'd never be popular. She didn't have the slightest idea how. So… she found other ways to be valuable to the community instead.

Despite the bustle, there was an air of solemnity. It was Sunday, the day to formally worship *Gott*. Socializing would come later, after the service.

Jane spotted Sarah and Rhoda, but there wasn't time to speak with them before the community filed into the Millers' barn and found places on the benches. She spotted Levy carrying Mercy, the only one on the men's side holding a baby. He gave her a nod and settled down on a bench.

Jane found it very coincidental that the deacons settled on the biblical theme of service and how to use one's gifts to the service of *Gott*.

Jane's gifts—of soothing babies, of being "useful"—sometimes seemed like curses. Over the years, she'd struggled with a defiant spirit that rebelled against being plain, against the expectation from others that she enjoyed the hard work, that she never minded the times romantic dreams took a back seat to utility.

But there were times she longed to stop being viewed as merely useful and start being viewed as a woman with hopes and dreams of a family of her own. None of that was possible if she shrank from meeting new people.

Her friend Rhoda said it best at the barbecue a few days earlier. *"That's why I think you should keep coming to singings and other youngie events,"* she had advised. *"How else will you get to know anyone?"*

So she sat and listened to the sermon and grappled with the awkward longing to get to know more people, which fought against the biblical call to service.

The worship service ended and people rose from their benches, stretching and talking.

Rhoda beckoned her over into the yard before the meal started. "Come here, Jane! I want you to meet some people."

Jane hesitated, fighting a desire to avoid the laughing, chattering groups. But she mastered her reluctance and prepared herself to endure her inevitable lack of social graces.

Rhoda introduced her to more young people their age, pulling her toward the more gregarious of the bunch. She received numerous invitations.

"We're having a barbecue—can you come?"

"I'm going to the singing next week, will you be there?"

"Everyone's going to the hot dog roast at the Herschbergers', can you make it?"

Jane smiled through clenched teeth. Of *course* she

would attend all these events. How else would she get to know anyone? And if a young man among the group should ever see beyond her glasses and plain features, perhaps she might have a hope for a family someday. The only way that would happen was if she forced herself to become a social butterfly.

At last she excused herself from the group and caught up with her aunt. She began bringing food out of the kitchen to the long tables set up under the shade of some trees.

"It's too nice a day to be inside. I'm glad we're eating outdoors." Jane placed a platter of fried chicken next to a bowl of potatoes.

"*Ja*, it's been so warm lately." Catherine wiped a bead of sweat from her forehead with a corner of her apron. "It looks like you've made some friends."

"I'm trying. I've received a lot of invitations."

"That's *gut*. You're a bit on the shy side, child, so going to social gatherings will help."

"I hope so. Everyone seems very nice." Jane bit her lip. "I just feel so awkward. It was bad enough back in Jasper, so why did I think it would be easier here, with a bunch of strangers?"

"It's putting you outside your comfort zone, for sure and certain," chuckled Catherine.

Jane remembered Levy using that very phrase when it came to learning salesmanship at the farmer's market. "*Ja*. That's exactly it. When will that end?"

"I don't know, but perhaps you'll meet a special young man at one of these gatherings."

"Don't get your hopes up." Jane spoke with a tartness she hadn't intended. "I'm sorry," she added.

Her aunt smiled. "I think things will get easier for you the more you go."

"I'm sure you're right."

"Come now." Aunt Catherine gestured. "Let's eat. People are starting to sit."

Everyone except Levy. Jane saw him at the edge of the large yard, standing under a tree, gently bouncing the baby. He looked ill at ease. Jane thought about taking over the care of little Mercy, and her conscience stung as she justified not following through. It was her day off, after all. And Levy had gotten enough baby lessons from her that he should be able to wrestle with his tiny bundle of responsibility.

Shouldn't he?

Juggling the baby in his arms, Levy watched the young people gathering around Jane. It concerned him to see her mingling with so many *youngies*. From where he was, he couldn't tell if she was enjoying it or not. He realized he didn't want Jane to be popular among her peers. Popularity wasn't necessarily a good thing.

His sister, Eliza, had been a popular young woman, and look what had happened to her.

He fought the instinctive reaction down. Jane wasn't like Eliza. She was a baptized member of the church, while Eliza was not. Still, it worried him.

Mercy stiffened in his arms, and her tiny face screwed up. She began to wail. Levy unslung the diaper bag from his shoulder and seated himself on the grass, rummaging for a bottle of formula. The minute the tip was in her mouth, she stopped crying.

Despite himself, he softened. Caring for a baby was a lot more work than he'd ever anticipated, but it had its redeeming moments. This was one of them. He even fancied he could see a resemblance to Eliza in the infant's features.

Did his sister think about what she was missing? Did she regret not seeing Mercy's first smile, her first step, her first word…

It was hard to think about that. He said a silent prayer for his sister's health and safety.

"There, little one," he crooned.

"You're getting good at that," said a voice.

Levy looked up to see Peter Troyer, Jane's uncle. "I don't have much choice." He lifted the baby into his arms.

"Seems like you're getting more comfortable holding her," Peter chuckled. "Though it was definitely an odd sight, having a baby on the men's side during worship."

"I felt pretty funny about it," admitted Levy. "But it's not as if I could ask Jane to take the baby for me. She's entitled to a day off like anyone else."

"I'll admit, Catherine said she was itching to give you a hand. But sometimes a man has to just cope, no matter whether it's babies or crops, ain't so?"

"*Ja.*" Levy bounced the baby. He liked Peter Troyer. He was a solid man who never shirked his responsibilities, and managed to keep a twinkle in his eye and a grin on his face. "I'll admit, this little one has her good and bad moments. When she's not crying, she's cooing. It melts the heart."

"It's *Gott*'s way of keeping us from doing our children harm," chuckled Peter. "Come, we're deciding on the Church Sunday hosting schedule. We need your voice."

Levy drove his buggy home with Mercy asleep in the basket he used as a traveling cradle. He'd gotten through the entire church service with minimal fussing on the part of the baby. He was rather pleased by this accomplishment. Maybe Jane's baby lessons were sinking in.

The *boppli* remained asleep as he parked the buggy in the barn and unhitched the horse. Not until he entered the house did she open her blue eyes. She wasn't quite ready to smile yet—she was too young—but that would come soon enough.

"*Ach*, *liebling*, I need to think what to do with you," he murmured to her as he lifted her from her basket to the bouncy seat on the kitchen table. He sat down in front of her and toyed with her tiny foot. "What's a bachelor uncle going to do with a baby girl?"

He always thought his adult life would follow the usual course of events—courtship, marriage then babies. But here he was, unmarried and with a baby to care for.

The usual twist of agony at the thought of his sister's fate hit his gut. After their parents had died in that horrible buggy accident, he honestly thought he could handle raising Eliza. At eighteen, he believed he was grown up enough to handle the responsibility.

But Eliza's headstrong behavior taught him differently. Never easy to handle, the grief of losing her parents at the age of twelve meant she no longer had the steady guiding hands of their mother and father to rein in her rebellious nature.

That's why seeing Jane surrounded by *youngies* at the Sabbath service disturbed him. All he could see was his sister…until she was gone.

And now… He tickled Mercy's little foot. And now Eliza had a baby she couldn't raise, and he had her baby who he refused to give up. It was all very confusing and frightening.

What was a bachelor uncle to do, indeed?

Jane showed up at Levy's farm bright and early one morning a few days later. She felt refreshed by the sunny weather. But Levy, she soon found out, had gotten out of bed on the wrong side.

"Just overwhelmed, I guess," he replied when she asked what the matter was. "I have so many things to do. Here." He thrust Mercy into her arms. "I'm already late milking the cows." With that, he stalked out of the house.

Jane stared after him. Perhaps it was her imagination, but it seemed his moodiness sprang from a different reason than his workload.

She gently bounced the baby. "Your uncle is cranky this morning." She touched the infant's nose. "But I'm not going to let him get to me. C'mon, I suspect it's time to wash some diapers."

Jane washed and hung the baby's laundry, then gathered other dirty clothes, swept the house, fed Mercy, put her down for a nap and made lunch. Whatever the cause of Levy's attitude, she would respond by making him a good meal.

She did not, however, eat lunch with Levy. She settled in the living room rocking chair to feed Mercy a bottle of formula.

He didn't say a word, either before or after the meal. Instead, he finished eating, put his plates in the sink and went back to work. As Jane washed the dishes, she looked out the kitchen window and noticed the raspberry bushes loaded down with fruit. She knew how difficult it was to keep up with berries when they peaked.

Picking up Mercy and tucking her in the sling, she descended into the cellar. "Let's go look for canning jars," she told the baby.

The high windows in the home's foundation gave dim light, and Jane was gratified to find hundreds of empty canning jars, which doubtless had belonged to Levy's mother. She picked up a box holding a dozen jars and brought them back upstairs. Then she took a bucket, went out to pick raspberries and came back in to set about making raspberry jam.

In the midst of the hot and sticky process, Levy suddenly entered the kitchen. "I owe you an apology, Jane," he stated without preamble.

Stirring the boiling jam, Jane looked up and wiped a trickle of sweat off her forehead with the back of her hand. "Oh?"

"*Ja.* I worry about my sister, and sometimes I project my worries about her on to you. It makes me bad-tempered, and I'm sorry for that."

Now that she was a bit more familiar with his background, Jane understood his fears. "But I'm not your sister. And I'm not doing anything against the *Ordnung*."

"Neither did she, until she left. But she was always going to *youngie* events. I thought she was on the path toward baptism, but I was wrong."

Jane softened. He was clearly tormented over the fate of his sister, not Jane's social life.

"I have three sisters," she said. "If any of them disappeared into the *Englisch* world, I would be frantic with worry too. Do you want to talk about it, or is it too painful?"

"Too painful." He pinched the bridge of his nose, then dropped his hand. "How many *brüder und schwestern* do you have?"

"Five. Three sisters, two brothers. My older sister is married and expecting her first baby. I'm the second oldest. My younger sisters and my brothers, they're all teenagers." She smiled. "It's a lot for my parents to handle at once."

"Do you miss them?"

"*Ja*, sure, of course. But they're all *gut kinner*. They don't give my parents any trouble."

"Unlike my sister." He removed his hat, stared at the straw brim for a few moments then plopped it back on his head. "I need to get back to work." He stalked out the side door.

Watching him stride away toward the fields, Jane

wondered why he felt the sudden need to apologize. But she was right—if anything happened to her sisters, especially her younger sisters, she would be panicky. It seemed he bore a lot of guilt over Eliza's fate. It must have been difficult to try to be a parent at such a young age. She supposed she could understand his odd quirks of behavior. Besides, his moods were none of her business. She was here to watch the baby and make herself useful. Nothing more.

By the time the jam was ready to jar, it was time to start dinner. She strapped the baby to her bouncy seat on the kitchen table, ladled hot jam into sterilized canning jars and set them in a pot of water to boil and seal. Then she made a simple dinner of grilled cheese sandwiches and tomato soup.

Levy came in carrying two buckets of fresh milk, which he strained into oversize jars and set down in the basement to allow the cream to rise.

"I can make butter tomorrow if you have enough cream," Jane offered when he came back up.

"*Danke*. I think there's enough." He sniffed. "Dinner smells good. I'm starving."

While he ate, Jane lifted the jars of jam from the water bath and set them on a towel to cool.

"What inspired you to make jam?" Levy spoke with his mouth full.

"The amount of raspberries left unharvested. It seems sinful to let them go to waste."

"This time of year there are more raspberries than I can sell, and they have to be picked fresh for the farmer's market." He rubbed his chin. "Maybe I can sell your jam too."

"I can keep picking berries through the week, then, and make more jam. Be sure to build in the cost of the jars and lids, since they're yours. I found them in the basement."

"I'll split the money with you, then. My supplies, your labor."

"Deal."

She felt a tentative truce was in effect, so she sat down and reached for a grilled cheese sandwich. Between them, the baby rested in her seat, making small motions with her hands.

"May I ask you a question?" Levy asked as he spooned up some soup.

"*Ja.*"

"Why are you here? What I mean is, why did you decide to come to stay with your aunt and uncle?"

It was the last question Jane expected, and she nearly choked on her sandwich. "Why do you want to know?"

"Just curious. Is it a big secret or something?"

"*Nein… Nein*, not really."

He raised his eyebrows. "Yet it seems you left something behind in Ohio. Did I hire a woman of questionable background to watch Mercy?"

"Of course not." She looked away, then heaved a sigh. "The truth is, the man I loved married my best friend. End of story."

"Whoa. Sounds more like the beginning of a story to me."

"I would rather not talk about it. It's painful and it's

something I chose to leave behind me. It comes from having a best friend who was pretty. Very pretty. And that's all I'll say about the matter." She stood up. "In fact, it's time for me to go. Leave the dishes. I'll do them tomorrow. Mercy's been fed and diapered. See you tomorrow."

She practically ran from the room and down the porch steps. Walking toward her aunt and uncle's house, she was angry at how she'd handled his question.

Her heart was pounding like it was going to pop out of her chest. What did it matter if Levy knew about the reason why she came to Grand Creek? It was not, after all, a deep dark secret.

Yet she realized Levy was the last person in the world with whom she wanted to discuss her love life—or lack thereof. How awkward was it, after all, to discuss it with her employer? She had no intention of baring her soul to him.

Thoughts of Isaac receded as she began thinking more and more about Levy. Despite his stubborn refusal to give Mercy to another family to raise, he had many excellent qualities. He was hardworking, devout, loyal, clever, dedicated and—when he chose to be— kind. His rare smiles lit up his face and made her heart beat faster.

What did that matter to her? He didn't see her as anyone attractive or interesting. And she refused to engage her heart where it wasn't wanted. She did not intend to turn Levy into another Isaac, longing for a man who didn't see her as a woman but merely as a tool.

"What is the matter with me, *Gott*?" she whispered. She seemed to settle her interest on men who didn't— or couldn't—return the interest. Was she unlovable? Or was she destined only to love those who couldn't love her back?

Chapter Six

With some amusement, Levy watched Jane flee from the house. So she'd left her heart behind in Ohio, had she? Smiling, he shook his head at her embarrassment. And found himself curious about her.

He was determined to pry those secrets out of her one way or another.

He went about caring for Mercy—a bit more comfortable now, thanks to Jane's baby lessons—and barely paid attention to why he was so interested in Jane's past.

Because he *was* interested. Not just in her life before she got to town, but in her. She was a unique package, unlike any woman he'd met before. On the surface she seemed quiet and demure, even plain. But underneath? He sensed a strong streak of stubbornness and, more importantly, strength. Strength of character, strength of integrity. He admired that in a woman.

He grinned at Mercy as she tried out a tentative smile at him. She was certainly an adorable *boppli*. "Come, little one," he said as he gathered her up in his arms. "Let's think of a way to pry your nanny's story out of her, shall we?"

When she arrived at her aunt and uncle's, Jane found Catherine just making some tea. "*Gut'n owed*, how went your day?"

"Fine. Fine." Jane gulped.

Catherine looked at her. "What happened?"

"Oh nothing." Jane dropped down into a chair. "Except I dodged some questions from Levy about why I left Jasper and came here. It was…awkward."

Her aunt prepared a second mug of tea and placed it on the table for Jane. "Why was he asking?"

"It just came up."

Her aunt frowned. "Was he flirting?"

"No!" Her denial came too quick. "Of course not."

"Because if he was, you could do worse," continued her aunt. "Levy's a *gut* man."

"Tante Catherine, please. Don't play matchmaker."

"*Ja*, sure." Her aunt looked unconvinced. "But you're young and pretty, so it's normal for me to wonder who'd make a *gut* husband for you."

"Pretty? I'm nothing of the sort." Jane shoved her glasses back up her nose. "Don't you know lying is a sin?"

"I'm not lying, *liebling*. You just have no confidence in yourself."

"Maybe not." Jane toyed with the tea strainer in her mug. "Years of experience, I guess."

Catherine sipped her tea. "There's been no one special for you? No rides home from singings?"

"*Nein*." Jane laughed with the very tinge of bitterness that had concerned her mother. "And the ironic thing is, my gift from *Gott* is I'm wonderful with babies. I can soothe any baby. I figured that out when I started babysitting for neighbors. Then I began getting hired as a mother's helper for women who'd just had babies. I don't like to think it's *hochmut* that I'm so *gut* with *bopplin*, but it's my gift. That's why Levy asked me to care for little Mercy. But am I likely to have *bopplin* of my own? *Nein*…" Her voice rose.

"Jane, stop it." Catherine spoke sternly. "You're being melodramatic now. You don't know what *Gott* has in store for you, but it's not likely to be a life of minding other peoples' babies. You're only twenty-three. There's plenty of time yet."

"Easy for you to say…"

"Jane, do you remember your baptism?"

Startled at the abrupt change of subject, she stared at her aunt. "Of course."

"Do you remember what you promised during the ceremony?"

"*Ja*, sure, I remember."

"What *did* you promise?"

"To walk with Christ and His church, to remain faithful through life until death, to confess Jesus is the Son of *Gott*, to abide by the *Ordnung* and be obedient and submissive to it…" It wasn't hard to rattle off the vows she'd taken, even though her baptism had been four years ago.

"*Gut*. You do remember. Then why are you failing to keep those vows?"

Jane's jaw dropped open. "What do you mean?"

"I mean, you're fighting *Gott* every step of the way. You fought Him when Isaac married your best friend. You fought Him over coming here to stay with us. You're fighting Him now, by questioning your appearance and your talents."

Chastened, Jane remained silent while she tried to process her aunt's words. They stung. "So you're saying it's *Gott*'s will that I'm a spinster and likely to remain so?"

"I don't presume to know *Gott*'s will. But—this is the thing you're forgetting—*neither do you*."

Tears welled up again, and one large one slid down her cheek and onto the table.

Catherine's face softened. "You're impatient, child. You want it all now and aren't willing to wait for *Gott* to work according to His will, not yours."

Jane heaved a huge and shuddering sigh. "You're right, Tante Catherine. I *have* been railing against *Gott*. It's just been so hard watching my sister and all my friends get married. Isaac and Hannah were the last straw."

The older woman patted Jane's hand. "Don't think we aren't thrilled to have you stay with us, no matter what difficulties you left behind in Jasper. But that's all behind you now. You have a whole new life to look forward to here. You need to have more confidence in yourself, child."

"I guess." Jane wiped her eyes. "I can't help but wonder if the people I've met so far are just being friendly because I'm new in town."

"Nonsense. You're not making friends out of pity, you're making friends because people like you. New friends are *gut* to have. I'm glad to see you so outgoing."

"It's a struggle," Jane admitted. "But Rhoda—she's one of those new friends—told me I wouldn't get to know everyone unless I went to *youngie* events. She's right. I know I have to get out more, even if Levy doesn't think so."

Her aunt raised her eyebrows. "Levy doesn't think it's good for you to have friends?"

"Well *nein*, he didn't quite say that. But he admitted he was projecting his sister's behavior on me. He apologized later and said he kept thinking about how his sister was so sociable right before she disappeared."

Catherine looked thoughtful. "*Ach*, poor man. And poor Eliza. He's right, she was very sociable. I think he believes that's when she started going down the wrong path. Most of the problem is he doesn't know where she is or what she's doing. The fact that she sent a baby for him to raise breaks his heart because he worries that the worst possible fate has befallen her."

"I had a lot more sympathy for him after I envisioned how I would feel if any of my sisters left the community." Jane sighed. "My problems seem a lot less important by comparison. I'll try to have a better attitude, Tante. I don't know what *Gott* has in store for me, but I'll try to be more patient."

Levy found himself looking forward to seeing Jane the next morning. He was determined to learn something about this mysterious past she'd alluded to.

But that would have to wait. He had work to do, and he felt the familiar stress arise as Mercy seemed inconsolable that morning, wailing without end.

Jane entered the house without knocking. "I could hear her crying from the road," she observed. "Apparently those baby lessons I've been giving you haven't sunk in yet."

He handed over the baby, and as if on cue, Mercy quieted down right away. He shook his head. "I don't know how you do it."

"Then you need more lessons." She gave him a cheerful smile. "Is there anything special you'd like for lunch?"

"Uh, no…" He thrust a hand through his hair. "You seem chipper this morning. Are you feeling okay?"

"Never better." She gave him a sunny smile and turned toward the kitchen. "If I'm making butter this morning, maybe I'll use some of it for biscuits with lunch. Biscuits and gravy. And maybe a potato casserole too."

"*Ja*, that sounds *gut*." He gave her a puzzled look and left the kitchen.

All morning as he hoed and weeded and picked and cultivated, he wondered about her change in attitude. Yesterday afternoon she seemed anxious. Today she was cheerful. What a mercurial woman she was.

"The man I loved married my best friend," she'd said yesterday.

Evidently that had been painful enough to send her fleeing from the security of her hometown, her parents and siblings, her church.

He found himself wondering just how attached she still was to this man she'd loved.

Before he knew it, it was lunchtime. When he returned to the house, he entered the kitchen and saw newly churned butter in a bowl on the counter, and fresh biscuits and gravy on the table. Jane was just pulling a potato casserole from the oven. Mercy sat quietly in her seat on the counter, watching Jane with large blue eyes.

"I don't know how you do it," he repeated as he washed his hands at the sink. "You get all this work done and Mercy stays quiet. With me, she never settles down."

"I'm sure part of it is because you're still nervous with her." Jane brought the bouncy seat and baby to the table, and placed Mercy in the middle as a centerpiece.

After the silent blessing, Levy reached for the biscuits. "So…why are you so cheery today?"

"I had a nice discussion with my *tante* yesterday after work," Jane admitted. She dished some potato casserole onto her plate.

"Does this have anything to do with the topic you avoided with me yesterday evening?" He split open the biscuits and ladled gravy over them.

He watched the changing expressions on Jane's face as some of her cheer seemed to evaporate. "I don't want to talk about it."

But Levy was determined to get her to open up—not just to satisfy his own curiosity, but because a small part of him wondered if his failure to listen to his sister's concerns when she was younger might have played a factor in her disappearance.

Jane was not like Eliza, of course. But perhaps she would like a sounding board just the same.

"So how long were you in love with that young man from your hometown?" he asked abruptly.

She glared at him. "Excuse me?"

"You heard me. How long were you in love with him?"

"Levy, that's none of your business."

"Maybe not, but don't you think it would be good to unburden yourself? You seem weighed down with something."

"I'm *not* burdened."

"Then why are you so defensive?" He took a bite of a biscuit.

"Because… Because…" He saw tears in her eyes.

He suddenly felt bad that her mood had taken a downturn, but he persisted. "Look, Jane, after seeing what happened to my sister, I think it's important to share burdens. It helps lighten the load. Won't you tell me?"

She stared at her plate, and Levy wondered if she would refuse to answer. Mercy gave a coo into the silence.

Finally she spoke in a low voice, still staring at her plate. "We went to school together, me, Isaac and Hannah. I had a crush on Isaac since I was, I don't know, maybe thirteen or fourteen. But he only had eyes for Hannah."

"Did he know how you felt?" Levy kept his voice gentle.

"Hannah is beautiful, and I'm... I'm not. I can't blame him for wanting to marry her."

Ah, so that was the crux of the matter. Jane thought she wasn't beautiful.

"And you think this Isaac only married your friend because she was prettier?" he persisted.

"It certainly was a factor in his decision. Why wouldn't it be?" Jane raised her head.

"If that was his only reason for marrying your friend, then he's a fool," proclaimed Levy. "Seems rather shallow."

"Maybe so, but what does it matter?" She shoved her glasses farther up on her nose. "It seems to be the way men think." She gave him a grim smile. "But you'd know that better than I would."

"*Nein*, I wouldn't. That's not the way I think." He saw skepticism on her face and continued, "You know very well *Gott* only sees the inside of a person, not the outside."

"*Ja*, sure. I'm grateful beyond words too, or I'd be in trouble. But it also meant Isaac only had eyes for Hannah, not me. And I didn't realize how much that hurt."

"And so you came here."

"My *mamm* said I needed a change of scenery because I was growing bitter and cynical."

"And what do you think of Grand Creek so far?"

"From what I've seen, I like it. Everyone seems very friendly. Speaking of which," she added, in a clear attempt to change the subject, "I've been invited to a hot dog roast this evening."

Instantly stress flooded through him as the implication sank in. "Oh. That means I'm in sole charge of Mercy."

"I'm sure you'll do fine."

"It's not just her physical care, though you've seen how bad I am at that. But I was going to work later into the evening and try to get a jump on things."

"In other words, you want me to work late." There was a touch of annoyance in her voice.

"*Nein... Nein*, I didn't say that…"

"Look, would it help to take Mercy with me?"

"Take a baby to a *youngie* event?" He raised his eyebrows.

She took another bite of casserole, then tickled Mercy's feet. "At this age, she shouldn't be much trouble."

"Are you sure? Because I'll freely admit, it would be a big help if you did."

"*Ja*, why not? If nothing else, it will be an experiment to see how she does. And since I've been invited to a singing on Friday, if tonight works well, I'll bring Mercy again. That way you'll be completely free to do whatever you need to get ready for the farmer's market."

"You're turning into quite the social butterfly." He didn't want to admit why Jane's popularity bothered him.

"It isn't easy, believe me." She looked at her plate. "I'm shy by nature, but I want to get to know people. It gets me…" She raised her head, and he saw a twinkle of humor in her eyes. "It gets me outside my comfort zone."

He remembered telling her that's what he had to do while selling his produce at the farmer's market.

"*Ja*," he agreed. "If you can take Mercy, you could combine business with pleasure. You can attend your *youngie* events, and I can get some work done."

"Are you finished? I'll wash up." She rose.

"*Ja. Danke*, lunch was delicious." He snatched up his hat and stepped out the door.

Back in the fields, he grabbed a hoe and applied it to the weeds. He realized he was discomfited by Jane's plans. But he was in no position to question her social life.

He tried not to think of his sister's popularity and where it had ultimately led. But Jane wasn't Eliza. He didn't have responsibility for her, not as he'd had with Eliza.

The fact that he had messed up when raising his sister was something he tried not to dwell on.

But it wasn't always easy.

Before she left for the hot dog roast, Jane packed a diaper bag with everything she could possibly need for the infant. She made dinner for Levy. She folded diapers and stacked them near the baby's crib. With Mercy tucked in the sling, she swept the house and porch.

When she was ready to leave for the event, she carried the baby and the diaper bag out to the barn where Levy was milking the cows. "I'm leaving now. I'll be back no later than 8:30. Your dinner is in the oven, warming. Don't worry about the dishes. I'll do them in the morning."

He barely looked up from his task. "Fine. Have fun."

She shrugged and set out for the function. Whatever Levy's issue with her attending *youngie* events, he couldn't fault her for neglecting her job.

The hot dog roast was held at the farm of Sarah's parents. Sarah was the first to spot her when she arrived. "You came! Oh, let me see the baby. Isn't she darling!"

Mercy was passed from person to person and cooed over. "She's so cute."

"What a joy!"

"She's such a quiet baby!"

Mercy didn't cry during any of these exchanges. When she finally found her way back into Jane's arms, Jane settled the baby in the sling and joined Sarah and Rhoda around a pit fire, where everyone held hot dogs on forked sticks over the fire.

"Is Levy glad you took the baby with you tonight?" asked Sarah.

"I guess. He's not pleased I'm here at all."

Her new friend looked surprised. "Why not?"

"I don't know. He acts like a bear with a sore paw whenever I mention coming to any singings. He seems to think I'm acting like his sister did before she disappeared."

"Levy's so *serious*," observed Rhoda. "And you're just the opposite. How do you two get along?"

"By not seeing each other much during the day. He's outside working, I'm taking care of Mercy in the house. End of story."

Sarah raised an eyebrow. "Any sparks between the two of you?"

"Lots. But not the kind you mean. There are times he drives me crazy, other times he's amazing to watch in action, like when he's at the farmer's market. Then it's like he's a different man."

"In a good way or a bad way?"

"Just a different way. He becomes far more animated, jokes and banters a lot with the customers and sells like crazy."

"He's interesting, all right." Sarah bit into a cookie. "I don't know him very well, but I've never heard anything bad about him. No one blames him for what happened with his sister. We all know he did the best he could with her."

"Maybe that's why he gets bothered when you attend *youngie* events," remarked Rhoda. "He's used to acting like a father."

"Well, he's not *my* father," Jane said as she laid Mercy on a soft blanket on the ground.

"*Nein*, but he's used to being a father to his sister. That's probably why he does it." Rhoda looked down at Mercy. "I wonder if Eliza will ever come back for her baby?"

"Did you know her?"

"Eliza? Of course. Everyone knew her. She was quite the social butterfly."

"That's the term Levy used with me," said Jane. "What was she like? Besides being a social butterfly, as you called her?"

"She was always laughing, always smiling, but she didn't much like working hard. Except sewing. She was very *gut* at sewing. Levy works all the time, so he used to get frustrated at her laziness. She kept up the garden pretty well, but I remember seeing the inside of their house once, and it was dusty and she had dirty clothes in her room. She didn't like cooking either." Sarah rubbed her chin. "I mean, neither do I, but that doesn't mean I won't do it. She was very stubborn about not doing things she didn't like. But with just the two of them, her and Levy, there's a lot to do even on a small farm. Maybe that's what drove her away, thinking she would have it easier if she lived among the *Englisch*."

"I wonder if she'll ever return to Grand Creek," Jane murmured.

"I think part of him thinks she won't," said Sarah. "That's why he's so determined to keep the baby. Maybe he feels he shouldn't fail the second time around."

"Yet I'm doing all the work with her." Jane tickled Mercy under the chin.

"I admire that you're nannying her," commented Sarah.

"What do you mean?"

"I mean, I think it would be hard to be a nanny, especially to a *boppli* this adorable. What if you fall in love with her? You're not her *mamm*. It's just a job. When the time comes, you'll move on, and what will happen to Mercy then?"

Shaken, Jane looked at the happy infant cooing on the blanket. "You're right. And it would be very easy to fall in love with her. But what choice do I have? What choice does Levy have? He can't take care of her by himself, not if he wants to be able to work."

"*Ja*, it's a problem all right." Sarah dangled a leaf over the baby's face, though Mercy couldn't quite focus on it. "It would be hard, in some ways, if Eliza ever *did* come back. It wouldn't be so hard now since Mercy is too young to know any different, but what would happen if Eliza came back when Mercy was older?"

Sarah spoke nothing but the truth—and where did that leave her, Jane? She hadn't planned on staying with her aunt and uncle forever. She missed her own family.

But leaving Mercy would mean depriving the baby of the only mother figure she'd known. With unease, Jane wondered if it wouldn't be better to leave sooner rather than later, before Mercy would know the difference. If Levy was determined to raise his niece, then he'd better take to heart those baby lessons.

"I think we're going to have rain tomorrow." Rhoda pointed overhead at the darkening sky. "Maybe even tonight. That's *gut*, we need it."

"I should probably get going." Jane rose to her feet. "I told Levy I'd bring Mercy back home by 8:30 so he could put her to bed."

"Are you coming to the singing on Friday? It's at my house," urged Rhoda.

"I hope so. I'll probably have to do the same thing and bring Mercy with me, but I'd like to attend."

"Everyone is so glad you're here," Rhoda stated. "We want you to come to every gathering!"

She smiled her thanks. "I'll come as often as I can. Come on, little one, let's go see your uncle." She lifted Mercy off the blanket and slipped her into the sling. "*Gude nacht.*"

She walked the half mile or so back to Levy's home. The clouds overhead thickened and a wind gusted up. Jane picked up her pace.

She hesitated at Levy's front door. Lamplight shone from within. She knocked before walking in. "Levy? I've brought Mercy home."

Levy emerged from the small room he used as an office. "*Ja, danke.*"

"Do you want me to change her diaper before I go?"

"*Nein*, I'll take care of it." His face was a neutral mask. He didn't ask her about the gathering, didn't ask how Mercy had behaved. He simply held out his arms to take the baby.

"I'll be here tomorrow then." Feeling peeved, she hung the baby sling on a hook by the door and left.

Would it kill Levy to show any warmth or appreciation? Would it pain him to inquire how her new friends were or how many people had attended the hot dog roast? As she stomped down the road, she admitted his lack of interest bothered her.

Levy didn't see Jane disappear into the night. He saw his sister Eliza walk away. For one moment, the two women merged in his mind, and he shook his head to dispel the illusion.

He knew he was projecting his fears and concerns about Eliza's behavior on to Jane, and that wasn't fair.

He looked at the sweet baby in his arms. She looked ready for sleep, her eyes just about drooping. He searched her features again for any traces of his sister, and believed he saw a similarity. Or was he imagining things?

He sighed and went about preparing Mercy for bed. How much did the baby resemble her father?

He shied away from speculating on the circumstances of Mercy's birth. He loved his sister with a fierce devotion, a bond made stronger after he stepped into the role of guardian when his parents died. His failure to rein in Eliza's wild adolescence weighed on him like a stone. He still blamed himself for her departure.

If Mercy was born out of wedlock as he suspected, then Eliza might never return to the community.

Yet he desperately hoped that one day Eliza would return to claim her baby, even if it meant facing down the inevitable gossip. That, more than anything else, accounted for his stubborn refusal to give Mercy to another family to raise. However irrational, Mercy was a link to his lost sister. If he gave up Mercy, he gave up all hope of seeing Eliza again.

He kissed the *boppli*'s forehead and laid the sleepy infant in her crib. He would never give up Mercy, because he would never give up hope that Eliza might return.

Chapter Seven

In the morning Jane opened her eyes and saw it was raining, no surprise after the change in weather she saw the night before.

"It is a gift from *Gott*, as we need the rain," Uncle Peter commented at breakfast, sipping coffee and looking at the gray weather outside.

"It's going to keep Levy indoors, though," muttered Jane.

Her uncle raised his eyebrows in a silent question.

She explained, "I've come up with a daily routine with the baby, and he's likely to get in the way."

"Well, it's his house. And his niece."

"*Ja*, I know." Jane scrubbed a hand over her face. "I'm sorry, Onkel Peter. It's just that…well, Levy and I don't always get along."

"He has a lot on his mind."

"I know, so I try to be understanding about it." Jane glanced at the clock. "But I'd better get going. I try to be there by seven."

Donning a cloak and taking an umbrella, Jane headed out toward Levy's house. The fields around her, even under a gray sky, greened up as the rain washed away dust and soaked the thirsty soil. Jane breathed deeply in the moist fresh air and vowed to keep her temper in check today.

Surprisingly, Levy was feeding the baby when she arrived, sitting with Mercy in the rocking chair as she drank a bottle of formula. "*Guder mariye*," she said. "Do you want me to take over?"

"*Ja*, please. I haven't milked the cows yet."

Mercy fussed when the bottle slipped out of her mouth, but Jane traded places, settled into the chair and continued feeding her. "You milk three cows, right?"

"Right. It takes me about half an hour."

"Have you had breakfast?"

"*Ja*." He crammed his hat over his curly hair. "Back in a while." He left for the barn.

When he returned with buckets of fresh milk, Jane was in the kitchen putting together lunch, with Mercy secure in the sling against her chest.

Levy stood in front of the sink, staring out the kitchen window at the pouring rain. "I won't get much done today," he muttered.

"Is it such a bad thing to take a day off?" Jane asked.

"I already have a day off," he replied. "On the Sabbath. The rest of the time, I'm on a tight schedule to get everything done in time for Saturday's market. You know that."

"Unfortunately, it doesn't look like you have a choice." She gestured toward the window.

"I know."

"Don't you have anything that needs doing in the barn?" she hinted.

He quirked an eyebrow at her. "Trying to get rid of me?"

"Well, *you* may not be able to work, but I'm still on the clock. And you're in the way." She tempered her words with a half smile, but truthfully her schedule was easier without Levy's constant hovering—even if it was, as her uncle pointed out, his house.

He moved away from the sink. "What is it you do all day?"

"What I always do," she retorted. "But normally you're outside."

"*Ja, ja*, you're right. I'm sorry, that was a *schtupid* thing to say." He shrugged. "I'll be in the barn."

What is it you do all day? In the now-silent kitchen, Jane snatched up dirty dishes and dumped them in the sink.

Whatever he found to do in the barn only kept him occupied for an hour, then he was back in the house. Jane pushed aside a strand of hair that had escaped her *kapp* as she chopped bell peppers and onions for a casserole. "Are you up for a trip to town?" she asked.

"*Ja*, I suppose. What do you need?"

"Formula for Mercy. We're running low."

"And it would get me out of the house, right?"

"Why yes, it would." She smiled and kept chopping.

"I have a few other things I could pick up as well. *Ja*, I'll go into town."

He grabbed his wallet and headed back for the barn. Jane sighed with relief.

Why was he so restless today? Whatever the cause, she was glad when she heard the clip-clop of hooves pull away from the house.

Levy hitched up his favorite mare, Maggie, to the buggy and swung into the seat.

He felt so restless today. He also couldn't believe he'd insulted Jane in such a way. *What is it you do all day?* How dumb could he be? He knew exactly what she did all day.

He trotted the horse toward the center of town.

His errands were trivial, but he lingered in the hardware store. He avoided the Troyers' dry-goods store.

It was with some relief that he saw friends hailing him from under a café awning where they lingered over coffee.

"Do you have time to join us?" asked Thomas.

"*Ja.*" Levy dropped into a chair. "This rain is keeping you from working outside too?"

"For sure and certain." Thomas winked. "And *alle daag rumhersitze macht em faul.* Sitting all day makes one lazy. I could be doing things in the barn, but I blame Paul here for dragging me into town on the pretext of going to the bank. Next thing I know, I'm drinking coffee."

Levy chuckled. He'd known Thomas Lapp and Paul Yoder since they were boys. They always managed to cheer him up, no matter what.

"How goes fatherhood?" asked Paul.

A waitress took his order and departed. Levy removed his hat and hooked it on the back of his chair. "Better, now that Jane's doing most of the hard work."

"Babies can be tough." Thomas tugged his beard. "My Annie, she juggles both our young ones very well, but it is definitely easier with two people at hand."

"Our third is due in about a month." Paul sipped his beverage. "Louisa is wonderful with the kids. My eldest boy, he's now old enough to follow me around the farm. He's a joy, as is my little girl. But tiny babies… they're best left to the *frauen*."

Thomas chimed in. "Have you considered giving Mercy to another family?"

Levy shook his head. "*Nein*. She stays with me. She's all I have of Eliza."

"Then it's good you have Jane to take care of her. Everyone says she's wonderful with babies." Paul grinned. "Better than you!"

The words were meant to be teasing, Levy knew, but they still stung. He drew his brows together. "So I'm a little awkward with Mercy. I haven't had any practice before this."

"Will Jane stay? Does she seem content to be Mercy's nanny?"

"*Danke*," Levy said to the waitress, who placed a coffee cup before him. "*Ja*, she says so. At this point I don't know what else I can do but keep her on."

"Why, is there a problem?" Thomas's brows arched upward. "Everyone talks well of her. Is she hard to get along with?"

"*Nein*, not exactly," Levy hedged. "I'm paying her

a little extra to handle housekeeping chores as well, and she's been very good about it. It's just that…" He stopped and stared out at the downpour just outside the café awning.

"Just that what?" prompted Paul.

"I don't know," he went on. "I can't put my finger on what's wrong. She's always wanting to go to singings and get-togethers. Last night she went to a hot dog roast and took Mercy with her. I can't say she's neglecting her job because she's not. It's just that…"

"…that you're thinking of Eliza," finished Thomas.

Levy felt his face flush. "It's true," he admitted.

"Is that a good enough reason to work against the best interests of the baby?"

Levy scowled. "I'm *not* working against her best interests. Jane's doing a fine job with her."

"But what are Jane's plans?" persisted Thomas. "You hired her right off the train, and she started working because she knew you were desperate. But she's under no obligation to stay. She can do whatever she wants."

Paul chimed in. "Remember, she's young and single, and there's no reason she shouldn't enjoy herself by socializing with other *youngies*." His expression altered. "Why do you object to her going to *youngie* events so much?"

"I don't."

Thomas chuckled. "Don't you know lying is a sin, Levy? Why does it bother you when she has some fun, especially since they're all chaperoned events?"

Levy remained silent, since he had no real answer for Thomas's question. He took another sip of his coffee.

Eager to change the subject, Thomas asked, "How goes the farmer's market sales?"

Levy was grateful for the conversation shift, and a few minutes later, they all parted ways.

He left his horse hitched out of the weather in the open-sided shed provided by the café and ducked into a small grocery store to buy formula for Mercy. He considered it bad luck when he bumped into Bishop Kemp.

"Ah, Levy!" exclaimed the venerable man. "I was going to call on you, but now I see you here."

"Bishop." Levy shook hands. "Quite the weather outside, ain't so?"

"*Ja*. I wanted to ask how it is with your sister's baby?"

"Uh, fine. Jane Troyer is doing an excellent job caring for her."

"*Gut, gut.* But Levy, you know that can only be a temporary solution." Bishop Kemp stroked his beard. "The *boppli* needs stability. Have you thought about getting married?"

"Married?" Levy's voice went high-pitched.

"*Ja*, of course. Married. That way the baby can have both a mother *and* a father."

"That's not a *gut* reason to get married." He scowled.

"Then you need to seriously think about giving Mercy to a family who can raise her." The bishop's voice was gentle and persuasive.

"That's not acceptable either." Levy scowled harder.

"Levy, are you listening to yourself? You're not being logical. You can't take care of her on your own—not if you have to work on the farm all day—so as I see it, you have three choices. You can get married, you can put her up for adoption or you can hire a succession of nannies."

Levy was silent, glowering.

The bishop continued. "Let me ask you this—why are you determined to keep Mercy? What's wrong with putting her up for adoption with another family?"

"She's all I have of Eliza."

"*Ja*, that's what you have said. So let me ask you a very, very hard question. Will you do a better job raising Mercy than you did raising Eliza?"

He stared, wide-eyed. "I don't know," he groaned.

Bishop Kemp laid a hand on Levy's shoulder. "I'm sorry to bring up such difficult things, my *sohn*, but you have to be practical. If you let her be adopted, nothing says you have to stay entirely out of her life. You can be as involved as you want. But the best thing you can give that *boppli* is stability…and you don't have that right now."

Levy's mouth pinched. "I know you're right, but it causes me physical pain to think about giving her away."

"Well, nothing must be decided right now. If Jane Troyer is doing as *gut* a job as you say, then you have time to think things through. But Levy, don't wait too long to decide. The longer you wait, the harder it will be on Mercy."

"*Ja*, I know." Levy squared his shoulders. "I'll give it some thought, Bishop Kemp. And meanwhile, I'll continue to pray for Eliza."

Levy purchased the formula, then returned to his

buggy. He unhitched Maggie and drove home through the rain.

"You're not being logical." Bishop Kemp's voice echoed in his ears as Levy reached home. He guided the horse into the barn and unhitched her, then spent more time than necessary grooming and feeding the mare. He oiled the harness and hung it on its hook. He even wiped down the buggy. Anything to avoid going into the house.

But when he could find no other excuse to putter around the barn, he placed his straw hat firmly on his head and walked into the house.

Jane was in the kitchen, which smelled of fresh-baked cookies. A huge platter of them rested on the table. She sat reading a book, a mug of steaming tea at her elbow.

"So *this* is what you do all day," he teased.

She raised her head. "*Ja.* That's after I made lunch, swept and dusted, did a load of laundry and hung it in the basement, and made cookies. Have one, they're oatmeal-raisin."

"*Danke.*" He picked one up and leaned against the counter while he ate it. "Is Mercy napping?"

"*Ja.*" She paused. "Levy, what's bothering you?"

"What makes you think something's bothering me?"

"You're jumpy as a cat today, and so critical. Have I done something wrong?"

The woman was too insightful. Not for anything would Levy confess his true concerns. "*Nein.*" He knew his voice sounded curt. "You've done nothing wrong. I, uh…have some things to do in the barn."

He fled the house.

* * *

Jane was far more upset by Levy's dark mood than she expected. Tears welled in her eyes, and she wiped them away.

Through the kitchen window she saw Levy pause in the doorway of the barn, just out of the relentless rain. Whatever "things" he had to do in the barn didn't seem urgent, as he simply stood there looking into the dark interior.

A grumble of thunder came from a distance, and still he stood motionless in the doorway. Jane admitted to herself why Levy's brusqueness hurt so much. She had begun to pin romantic hopes on the man where none existed.

"Jane, you *schtupid* fool," she whispered. "Wasn't Isaac enough? Do you need to get kicked in the shins by Levy too?"

It became very clear to Jane that she wanted Levy to see her as a woman, an interesting woman, an attractive woman...not a "useful" woman. But now, it seemed, even her usefulness was limited. *What is it you do all day?*

Through the window she saw him turn and head back to the house. She composed herself just before he opened the kitchen door and strode back in.

He filled the kettle and set it on the stove to heat, pulled out a mug and a tea bag, then sat down across the table from her. "Can we talk?"

"*Ja.*" She suppressed the shuddering breath that preceded a crying jag. "I want to know what I've done wrong."

"You haven't done anything wrong, Jane. I'm just worried about Mercy's future." He rubbed his chin. "I bumped into the bishop in town. He asked me why I didn't give Mercy to a family who could raise her. It's a lot harder than I thought to be her guardian, and now I'm questioning my decision. The bishop still wants me to reconsider."

"But you're stubbornly refusing to do what's right for Mercy."

"Yes, I am." His face grew stern. "I love my sister. I love her more than anything. A little frightened part of me is worried that if I give Mercy away, I'm giving away all hope of seeing Eliza again. I keep wondering where I went wrong with her, what I could have done differently."

"Levy." Jane stood up as the kettle started to sing. She poured water over his tea bag. "Will you tell me what happened with you and Eliza? How you came to take care of her? Explain to me why you're so determined to keep a newborn baby."

"How much have you heard from others?"

"Not much. Just some gossip. Everyone thinks highly of you, and even if they disagree with why you're keeping Mercy, they understand it."

Levy looked surprised. "That's *gut*, I suppose."

Jane sipped her tea. "All I know is you'd taken care of your sister since your parents died. She left, never came back and you only heard from her when she sent the baby into your care."

"That's the gist of it." Levy dipped his tea bag in and out of the cup, staring at the darkening water. "My parents died when a car hit their buggy. That was ten years ago. Eliza was twelve years old at the time, and I was eighteen. My parents only had two children. When they died, it was just Eliza and me."

"How did Eliza take your parents' deaths?"

"Very hard, as you can imagine. We both did, but she was at a more impressionable age. I stepped into a fatherly role for Eliza." He closed his eyes. "I guess I wasn't very good at it."

Filled with compassion, Jane touched his hand briefly. He opened his eyes and looked at the spot she'd touched.

"Up until about the age of fifteen, she was fine. I'd already been baptized, and I thought she was on the same path. A nice young man named Josiah was interested in her. But then she hit a rebellious phase, running around with other *youngies*, neglecting her chores, acting disrespectfully. I just didn't know what to do, how to cope." His voice trembled.

"My friend Sarah said she left on her *Rumspringa*."

"*Ja*, that's right. She was taking classes to be baptized, but one day while in town she met an *Englischer*, and next thing I knew she was gone. I can only presume Mercy is the result of that relationship. It…it kills me to think of Eliza, alone and pregnant…and all because I didn't know how to handle a teenage girl."

Jane tried to be sympathetic. "With *Gott*, all things are possible. Eliza may come around…"

Levy laughed bitterly. "And be accepted by the community? I don't think so."

"Don't be so sure. If she was never baptized, she

can still return and be forgiven for her sins. I think you might be too hard on her."

"Wouldn't you be?" He fixed her with an angry glare. "If you were in my shoes, could you speak so easily of forgiveness?"

"Maybe not." Jane sighed and took a sip of her tea. "I would be devastated if either of my two younger sisters followed the same course Eliza did. But you can't see into the future, Levy, nor can you change the past. If I were in a position to counsel you, I would tell you to forgive yourself for what happened in the past, and pray for what might happen in the future."

He pinched the bridge of his nose. "Why should *Gott* listen to me?" he muttered.

She was surprised to hear him say such a thing. "*Gott* always listens!"

"Then where is my sister?"

"*Gott* knows, and He's got His hand on her. Don't lose your faith, Levy—it's the most important thing you have."

"I'm trying not to." He stared at his mug. "But it's hard. I worry she's alone in some big city."

"The one thing to remember is Eliza is not a child any longer. She's a grown woman, and she's making her own way in life. It may not be a way you approve of, but it's her life."

"But not her child?"

"Maybe not."

Levy sighed. After a long pause, he asked, "Jane, that's another thing I wanted to ask—how long do you think you'll be able to work as Mercy's nanny? I need to think about Mercy's future, and that means finding out how long you anticipate staying."

"I don't know." She toyed with her spoon. "Originally I wasn't going to stay more than a few months. I like this community, I like the people I've met, I like my work, I love my *tante* and *onkel*…but I was born and raised in Ohio and want to keep the option of going home. But already I can see this will be a problem—not just because of my future, but because of Mercy's."

"So can you give me a deadline for when I should look for a replacement? Are you thinking two months? Three months? Four months?"

"It's too hard to predict. But one thing is certain. Without a mother in the picture, someone permanent, it's going to be hard having a series of nannies go in and out of her life."

"I know…"

Just then the infant started crying from the bedroom. Jane rose to her feet. "As I told you before, however long I'm here, I'll continue to care for Mercy as if she were my own." She bit her lip. "In fact, it will be hard to give her up when the time comes."

Chapter Eight

Jane changed the baby's diaper, then settled into the rocking chair to give her a bottle. She watched the baby as she drank. Her tiny hands looked like stars.

She'd told Levy the truth. It would be very hard to give Mercy up when the time came. She realized she was falling in love with this precious and sweet *boppli*.

"I think when your belly is full, I'm going to give you a bath," she crooned. The infant's large blue eyes gazed upward as she sucked on the bottle.

When the formula was gone, Jane placed a clean diaper over her shoulder and placed the baby over it, patting the tiny back until she emitted a satisfactory *braaap*.

When she returned to the kitchen, Levy was gone. Jane warmed some water and padded a washbasin with a towel. She filled the washbasin with hot and cold water until she was satisfied with the temperature.

"C'mon, little one, let's get you washed." Jane gathered clean clothes, a washcloth, a cup for rinsing and other accessories.

Mercy enjoyed the bath. She smiled and cooed as Jane soaped her little body, then rinsed her off, protecting her eyes with the washcloth. As she worked, Jane felt the warmth of love steal over her for this tiny *boppli*. No matter what her future held, it would be hard to stop caring for Mercy.

She dressed the baby, then placed her in her bouncy seat on the kitchen table. She started to cook dinner when she heard a knock at the door.

Picking up the baby, she went to answer. Her friend Rhoda stood on the porch, panting, a dripping umbrella at her side. "We're having another singing in the Millers' barn since it's too wet to work outside," she gasped, grinning. "I ran all the way over here to ask if you can come. It starts in an hour, and if you can come, bring something to eat since we'll all have dinner there."

"*Ja*, I think so. I'll have to make dinner for Levy, but that sounds like fun."

"*Gut*! See you there."

When Jane closed the door and returned to the kitchen, Levy was there, rain dripping off his hat brim. He looked at her unsmiling. Then he turned to wash his hands at the sink.

"I'll make double the amount of dinner and bring half with me to the singing tonight," said Jane.

"That's fine." He wiped his hands on the dish towel.

"I can bring Mercy with me, if you like."

"Great."

A wave of pity came over her. "Levy, I know you're upset by what the bishop said. But try not to worry about Mercy's future. *Gott* will provide."

"*Ja*." He looked down at the dish towel in his hands.

"I know. I've been praying for clarity, for guidance. I just don't see the right path yet."

"You will, I'm sure. And for the moment, Mercy's in *gut* hands." Jane patted the *boppli* on the back.

Levy looked at her, and she saw gratitude in his eyes. "Whatever happens in the future, I thank *Gott* I saw you that day at the train station."

Jane held his eyes a heartbeat longer than required before she dropped her own gaze. "*Ja.* Well, I guess I'll start dinner."

Levy disappeared into his office. The rain pattered on the roof, and Jane opened the kitchen window a bit to let the moist warm air into the house. She tried not to think of that vulnerable raw emotion she saw in his eyes. She tried not to dwell on how her own heart responded.

She set the table for Levy, packed the extra food into an insulated carrier and tucked it inside Mercy's diaper bag. Then she slipped the *boppli* into the sling, and put on her cloak to protect both of them from the rain. She stopped at the doorway to Levy's office, where a lamp lit the inside against the gloomy afternoon, illuminating an account ledger.

"I'll be leaving now. I've left dinner for you on the table."

"*Danke.* Have fun." He gave her an abstracted smile, then continued scratching in the ledger with a pen.

She picked up her umbrella and the diaper bag, and set out for the Millers' farm.

It pained her to see Levy hurting. And she wondered what else she could do to help this man, whom she was growing to care for.

* * *

She saw many young men and women walking toward the Millers', with umbrellas bobbing from different directions. The large barn doors were wide open in welcome. Jane stepped inside, shook the rain off her umbrella and stacked it near the doorway with dozens of others.

The Millers had set up boards across sawhorses along the outside walls of the main part of the barn. Jane joined the groups of chattering, laughing young people placing food along the boards. For such a spontaneously arranged function, a lot of people had come. The rain pounded on the roof overhead, but inside the barn the energy was high.

"What's wrong?"

Jane turned and saw Rhoda. "What do you mean, what's wrong?"

"You were standing there like you're angry."

"Oh, nothing. Just some moodiness from Levy, that's all." Jane gave Mercy a little bob in the sling, but the baby was cozy and alert.

"Is he still giving you grief about attending *youngie* events?"

"Not so much. But he's…" Jane trailed off. Gossiping was a sin, and she'd nearly gossiped about Levy's private struggle. "Well, he just has a lot on his mind," she went on.

Some others clustered around Jane, cooing at the baby, so she took Mercy from the sling and allowed her to be passed from arm to arm. Free of the infant, Jane found herself surrounded by several young men, who engaged her in conversation.

These were the same young men, she realized, who seemed to hang around every event she'd attended so far. Caught up in the notion she was plain, it dawned on her that she was, for the first time in her life, attracting male attention.

This was reinforced later when Sarah sidled up and whispered, "I think Charles is interested in you."

"What? Really?" Jane refrained from glancing over at the young man. "I thought it might be David, since he's been at my side the whole evening."

"Him too. And maybe even Daniel. But not Josiah. I thought he was too heartbroken still, but now he may be courting."

Josiah? Jane's ears pricked up. That was the young man Levy's sister had left behind when she disappeared into the *Englisch* world.

"Which one is Josiah?" she asked Sarah.

The young woman pointed to a nice-looking man with straight brown hair. He sat with another young woman, talking. "He was stuck on Eliza for a long time," Sarah stated. "But now maybe things will be different. I hope so. He's a *gut* man. Come on, the singing is just getting started."

The mishmash of chairs and benches filled up as the young people seated themselves, most with hymn books in hand. Jane took Mercy back and found herself with Sarah and Rhoda, while the young men seated themselves opposite, with Jane's admirers sitting as near to her as was possible in the barn.

The group sang vigorously for half an hour before breaking for something to drink, and Jane found herself once more the center of attention. She remembered telling Levy of the need to step outside her comfort zone, and she realized it was getting easier to do as she chatted with her new friends.

Jane noticed Josiah glance at her, then look away. She suspected it was because he knew she held Eliza's baby. He remained with the young woman she'd noticed earlier.

The group sang some more, then broke for the meal. Jane went into a quiet corner so she could change Mercy's diaper and feed her.

Sarah kept her company while the baby drank her bottle. "I saw Charles whispering to his brother and glancing your way," she confessed. "I wouldn't be surprised if he was thinking about courting you."

The thought was not exciting, though she liked Charles well enough.

Sarah's teasing grin faded. With feminine precision, she asked, "Is it Levy?"

"What? No!"

Her friend's eyebrows arched. "Well, then, is Levy interested in you?"

"As a nanny, yes. As a woman, of course not."

"What makes you so sure?"

"We're like oil and water. He doesn't like it when I attend *youngie* events, and I don't like his moodiness."

"Okay, if you say so." Sarah grinned.

"Stop it," ordered Jane. "Don't create something that isn't there."

"I don't think I have to." Sarah's eyes twinkled. "You say boys never paid much attention to you before, but why bother with boys if a decent man like Levy finds you interesting?"

To her annoyance, Jane felt her face flush. "He doesn't. He just finds me *useful*."

"And how do you feel about Levy?" Sarah asked her.

Jane looked down at Mercy. "It used to be I wanted to strangle him half the time. Now, that's not the case. I know he's wrestling with what to do with the *boppli*, and that means he's sometimes hard to be around."

"I can imagine. Is she done drinking her bottle? I saw some walnut brownies on the table."

Jane returned the empty bottle to the diaper bag and hoisted Mercy over her shoulder, burping her as she went. She joined Sarah in line for food.

And when Charles offered to carry her plate, citing her full hands with the baby, she thanked him and wondered what it would be like to be courted. By anyone.

The rain continued to fall as she set out to return to Levy's after the singing. It wasn't terribly late and the skies were gloomy, but not pitch-dark. Jane had no trouble seeing the road as she walked back. Mercy slept in the sling, snug against Jane's body.

As she approached Levy's house, she saw he had set a lamp in the window for her. That thoughtful gesture touched her.

She let herself inside, making sure to create a lot of noise so Levy knew she was back. Soon he emerged from the kitchen, coffee cup in hand, as she closed the door behind her.

"How was the singing?" he asked.

"It was fun. Lots of people." She paused for effect, then added, "Lots of cute boys too."

His mouth thinned. "How nice."

"And Sarah pointed out Josiah to me. It looks like he might be courting someone."

Levy nodded. "I'm sure that's for the best. He took Eliza's departure hard."

"He seemed to avoid me. I think it's because I had Eliza's baby with me." She patted the baby's bottom through the sling. "But everyone else loves her. She gets passed around and fussed over."

Jane made her way to the kitchen, where she placed the diaper bag on a chair. "I'm going to diaper and feed Mercy, then put her down. I think she's quite tired."

By the time the *boppli* was fast asleep in her crib, it was pitch-dark outside with the rain still falling. "I can drive you home in the buggy," offered Levy.

"*Nein, danke.* I know the way and can probably walk it quicker than it would take you to hitch up the horse." Jane swung her cloak around her shoulders and fastened the clasp. "I'll see you in the morning. Hopefully the rain will have stopped."

She picked up her wet umbrella from the porch and started walking toward her aunt and uncle's house. She was later than usual and hoped they hadn't worried.

"It was an impromptu singing," she explained after arriving home. "I'm sorry I didn't let you know, but it was so much fun!"

Uncle Peter chuckled. "This rain put off a lot of work today, so I'm glad the Millers donated the use of their barn for a singing."

Jane removed her damp cloak and hung it to dry on a peg near the front door. "I was happy to have something to do, since Levy was hanging around the house all day and driving me nuts."

Peter raised his eyebrows. "Does he often drive you nuts?"

"*Ja.* We seem to rub each other the wrong way."

Her uncle looked concerned. "Is it too difficult to work for him? You can come work in the store anytime, you know."

"*Nein*, I couldn't do that to Mercy. It would mean leaving her in the clutches of an incompetent uncle." She made a face, then chuckled. "Don't worry, Onkel Peter. Levy is outside in the fields most of the time anyway, and Mercy is a joy."

"Well, if you're sure…"

"I'm sure." Jane yawned. "*Gude nacht*, I'm off to bed." She kissed her aunt and uncle on their cheeks and went upstairs.

Jane woke to a day that dawned sunny and humid, with the earth giving off moisture after the relentless rain of the past few days.

As soon as Jane arrived at the farm, Levy was frantic. "I have tons to do," he said. "I missed a whole day of work yesterday, so I have to get moving if I'm going to have enough to sell at this week's market."

"Anything I can do to help?"

He paused and looked at her. "Would you be able to pick raspberries and work on jam? We can sell it on Saturday."

"Sure. It's not hard to do with a baby in the sling, or on a blanket in the shade."

"Then yes, that would be great. *Danke*."

He seemed to have gotten over his moodiness from yesterday, Jane thought. She fed and diapered the baby, tidied the house, then bundled Mercy in the sling, grabbed a blanket and a couple of buckets and headed outside to the raspberry patch.

The day was warm, and she was glad some of the patch was shaded by a generous maple tree. She stripped Mercy down to just her diaper and laid her on a blanket under the tree and picked nearly two gallons of berries before the baby got squirmy and Jane was sweaty.

"Wow, that's a lot of berries." Levy came around the corner of the house and peered at the buckets.

"It will certainly add to your inventory of things to sell on Saturday, once I get these turned into jam. Is it lunchtime already?"

"If my growling stomach is any indication," he joked, and just then, Jane's own stomach made noises. They both laughed.

He glanced at the baby. "It's not too hot out here for her?"

"No worse for her than for you or me." Jane leaned down and lifted Mercy, whose face was beaded with sweat. She wiped the infant with a corner of her apron. "But *ja*, she seems warm. I'm ready to go inside."

She slipped Mercy into the sling and picked up one of the buckets of berries. Levy grabbed the other and she followed him into the kitchen.

"It's just going to be sandwiches for lunch today."

She put the baby in her bouncy chair on the table and bustled around the kitchen, preparing food.

Levy washed his hands and made himself a sandwich from the ingredients Jane laid out. He sat at the table and looked at Mercy. "She seems awfully quiet today."

"She's probably just warm." Jane sat down and took a bite of her own sandwich. "She was quiet while I was picking raspberries, which was *gut*."

Levy gulped some cool water and finished his sandwich. He grabbed a few oatmeal-raisin cookies from the supply Jane had made yesterday. "I'm heading back to work."

Jane looked at the buckets of raspberries and sighed. Making jam was hot work, and it was already a hot day.

At least Mercy stayed quiet while she worked. It took all afternoon, but Jane preserved sixteen pints of jam from the berries she'd picked that morning.

She shoved a damp strand of hair off her forehead as she surveyed her handiwork, satisfied. The jars were lined up on the countertop, cooling on a towel. They looked like jars of rubies. That should bring in a nice bit of extra income for Levy—and herself.

She washed up and glanced at Mercy, who had fallen asleep in her bouncy chair. Jane frowned. The child looked flushed. She laid a hand gently atop the baby's forehead and nearly gasped at the heat she felt. Mercy had a fever! A high fever! While she was busy working on the jam, the infant entrusted to her care was burning up with fever.

Moving fast, Jane took some of the boiling water from the stove and poured it into the same washbasin she'd used to bathe the baby yesterday, then diluted it with cool water until the bath was just a bit cooler than tepid. She laid a padded towel into the water.

Then she unstrapped the baby and lifted her up. Mercy whimpered but didn't wake. Jane stripped her bare, then laid the baby into the water, pouring liquid over the heated limbs and belly. Mercy woke up, her eyes glazed with fever, but didn't cry.

"Please, *Gott*, let her get better," Jane whispered. "Please, *Gott*, let her get better…"

Guilt plagued her. If she'd only paid attention to the baby, not the jam, not her tangled feelings about Levy, not her own fatigue. The baby. Her sole focus should have been the baby.

Jane spent twenty minutes trying to cool down the child. At last she lifted her out of the water and wrapped her in a dry towel, then scoured the house for medicine, anything to lower her fever. She found nothing.

By the time Levy came back in from his work, sweaty and dirty, she was nearly frantic with worry. "Mercy's sick," she told him. "She has a high fever. Do you have any baby ibuprofen in the house?"

"*Nein*, I don't." Concern written on his face, he peered at the infant's flushed skin. "Should I hitch up and go buy some?"

"I think so, *ja*." Jane placed the baby over her shoulder and patted her back. "Whatever you do, make sure you don't get aspirin—babies can't have it. It should be ibuprofen. And if you're going out, can you stop at my aunt and uncle's and let them know I might not be home tonight? I want to stay with her."

"*Ja*." Levy snatched up the sweat-soaked straw hat he had just discarded and put it on his head. "I'll be back as quick as I can."

While he was gone, Jane bathed Mercy once again in cool water, praying the fever would lessen.

Levy came back much sooner than anticipated, panting. "We're taking her to the hospital," he said without preamble. "Catherine said fevers in babies this young are an emergency. Peter is asking an *Englisch* neighbor to drive us over there."

Panic clutched Jane at the thought of Mercy being in danger. "I'll pack a diaper bag."

She ran around the house, gathering bottles and formula and clean diapers and other necessary items. And all the while she berated herself for her lack of vigilance. If only she hadn't picked raspberries. If only she hadn't made jam. If only…

"Jane, calm down." Levy, still filthy from his outdoor work, watched her frantic movements.

She stopped in her tracks and covered her face with her hands. "Please, *Gott*, let her be okay," she whispered. She looked at Levy and felt the pressure of tears. "I feel like it's my fault she's sick."

"*Nein*, it's not. Babies get sick sometimes." He cocked his head toward the screen door. "I think I hear the car. Let the doctor tell us why she's sick before you start blaming yourself. *Komm*."

Chapter Nine

Levy carried the packed diaper bag and Jane carried Mercy, who wore nothing but a diaper and a thin blanket. Jane barely saw the car's driver, but she thanked him in a shaky voice for agreeing to drive them to the hospital.

"I've got kids. I understand," he said.

The driver raced through the streets until he reached Grand Creek's small hospital, and pulled right up to the emergency room entrance. Jane scrambled out right behind Levy.

"This baby has a high fever," Jane told the receptionist.

"Are you the mother?"

"No, I'm the nanny..."

"I'm the baby's uncle and her legal guardian." Levy spoke over her shoulder.

"The fever spiked up this afternoon," Jane told her. "I've been giving her cool baths but it's not making a difference."

A nurse came through the double doors. "How old is the baby?"

"She's about four weeks old."

The professional nodded. "It's good you brought her in. At that age, fevers can be serious. We'll check her for infection." Then the nurse whisked Mercy deeper into the hospital while Levy started filling out the inevitable paperwork.

Jane huddled on a waiting room chair, feeling helpless and vulnerable…and guilty. The baby's unusual lethargy should have tipped her off.

"Still blaming yourself?" Levy dropped into the seat next to her.

"*Ja*. I should have noticed she was sick sooner than I did."

"Funny, I've been thanking *Gott* you noticed as quickly as you did."

A doctor came out the double doors. "Mr. Struder?"

Levy jumped up. "*Ja*, that's me."

She smiled reassuringly. "I want to let you know what we're doing with little Mercy."

Jane stood up too. "Will she be okay?"

"Very likely. It's a good thing you brought her in right away. A baby's body is less able to regulate temperature than an adult's, so it can be more difficult for them to cool down during a fever. Their bodies are naturally warmer than an adult's body because they are more metabolically active, which generates heat. Was she in the sun much today?"

"I had her outside," confessed Jane, feeling miserable. "She was lying on a blanket on the grass, but it was fully in the shade all the time. A huge maple tree…"

"Then it's not sunstroke. Don't worry, having her in the shade outside didn't cause this to happen, so don't beat yourself up."

"We were at a singing a few nights ago," she recalled. "She was being passed around to a bunch of people who wanted to hold her. Could she have picked something up?"

"It's hard to say at this point," said the doctor. "By itself, a fever does not necessarily mean a serious illness. If the baby's behavior is normal, they're likely to be okay. But with infants this young, it's best to err on the side of caution."

"What will you test her for?" asked Levy.

"The biggest concern is meningitis," replied the doctor. "It's a bacterial infection of the membrane that covers the spinal cord and the brain. Untreated, it can be very serious. But if treated, recovery is almost always complete. I'm grateful you got her here as quick as you did. When babies get sick, they get sick fast."

"How long will she have to be here?" asked Jane.

"Until we get the tests run." The doctor looked at Levy. "You said you're the baby's legal guardian, yes? Where is the mother?"

"I don't know." Levy looked distressed. "I haven't spoken to my sister in years."

"So you don't know your sister's current medical condition?"

"No."

The woman continued, "I hope I'm not scaring you.

The good news is the vast majority of infants with fevers have mild infections like colds or stomach viruses that resolve in a few days without any problems. And the other good news is that even more serious infections are treatable. The earlier we start treating them, the better the chances the baby will be fine."

"So now we just have to wait?" asked Jane.

"I'm afraid so." The doctor looked sympathetic. "That's the hardest part, I know. There's a coffee shop just down the street if you're hungry, but otherwise you can make yourself comfortable in the waiting room."

After the doctor left, Levy looked at Jane. "Are you hungry?"

"I honestly haven't stopped to think about it."

"Well, I am." He plucked his shirt. "I'm also sorry I'm so dirty and sweaty, but appearances were the last thing on my mind. Still, I have some money in my pocket, so let's go get something to eat."

Jane walked with Levy to the air-conditioned restaurant and slid into a booth with a sigh. "I'm still beating myself up."

"That makes two of us." Levy removed his straw hat and placed it beside him on the booth seat. "I keep wondering…" He trailed off.

"Wondering what?"

"Wondering if I'm cut out to be a father."

"No one is cut out to be a father—or a mother— when it first happens."

"Then how do people do it?"

"They learn on the job, how else? The only difference between you and other people is you didn't have nine months to mentally prepare yourself like most dads do."

"True." He stared at the cutlery on the table. "This made me realize how much Mercy has come to mean to me. I've grown to love her so much. I suppose that's another thing new dads do."

"Of course." Jane closed her eyes for a moment. "I'm the same. She's such a lovable baby. Despite the oddness of how she arrived, it's like she was meant to be here."

When she opened her eyes, she saw Levy watching her. "That's something I hadn't thought of," he admitted.

"What's that?"

"That you—as the nanny—might fall in love with Mercy."

"I've taken care of a lot of babies over the years, but never as a full-time job. It's an occupational hazard I didn't anticipate."

"Then how will you—" He was interrupted by the waitress, who came to take their order. After she departed, Levy continued, "How will you handle it when it comes time for you to leave this job?"

"I don't know." Pain stabbed her in the heart at the thought of leaving Mercy…and Levy. "I haven't thought that far ahead. Falling in love with Mercy wasn't what I'd planned."

Levy sighed. "Life certainly has a way of becoming complicated. I'm a simple man. I prefer a simple life. I didn't anticipate something like this."

"It's been a stressful day," she acknowledged. "And depending on how long the tests may take, I think I'll spend the night here. You've got work to do on the farm, including milking the cows. I'm the logical person to stay with her."

He nodded. "I won't argue. I'm grateful, Jane. I don't know how I'd do this without you."

When the food was delivered, Jane bowed her head and prayed for Mercy's health. Then she unfolded her napkin and glanced around the restaurant. "I wonder how many people here have friends or relatives in the hospital."

"I don't like hospitals." Levy bit into his hamburger. "They remind me of when my parents were killed."

She couldn't imagine the pain Levy must have been through in his life. No wonder he was so adamant about keeping Mercy despite all the difficulties involved.

She looked at him, sitting across the table from her. He was not pleasing to the eye at the moment. His face was streaked with grime from the day's work, his shirt was filthy, his hair plastered to his head from the shape of the straw hat.

Yet he had strength and maturity in his face, a sense of purpose and determination. The burdens and responsibilities he took on in his life, he took very seriously.

She compared him to Isaac, and realized with a sense of shock that, next to Levy, Isaac was still a boy, at least in her memory. Levy was a man. And despite the dirty clothes and face, he was a handsome man.

She sighed as she took a bite of her own food. The last thing she needed was to start thinking about her boss in that way. She had enough on her plate right now—and so did Levy.

When they returned to the hospital, Mercy was still undergoing tests and the receptionist instructed them to be seated. An hour passed, then two. Finally a doctor emerged from the swinging double doors. "Mr. Struder?"

Levy bounced to his feet. "*Ja?*"

Jane rose too.

"I'm Dr. Forster." He shook hands with Levy, then Jane. "I want to let you know the baby is stabilized. We have her on an antibiotic IV drip and we've managed to control her fever. The good news is we've ruled out meningitis, which was the most serious threat."

"Thank *Gott*," whispered Levy, pinching the bridge of his nose.

"Do you know what caused the fever?" asked Jane.

"Are you the mother?"

"No, I'm the nanny."

"The baby's mother is my sister," explained Levy. "She is…well, I don't know where she is. A few weeks ago she sent the baby to me to raise. I hired Jane to care for her."

The doctor nodded. "That helps us decide a couple of things. I'll be honest, Mr. Struder. The baby may have a condition she picked up from her mother during the birth itself. Since we don't know your sister's prenatal health, we have to make sure the baby didn't pick up a pathogen of some sort. This can mean mild symptoms for the mother, but much more serious implications for a baby."

Levy paled. "How serious?"

"Try not to worry." The doctor held up a hand. "Much

of what we're doing is ruling out what she *doesn't* have. But because newborns with high fevers can be at risk, we tend to be pretty aggressive in our evaluation and treatment. So far we've ruled out meningitis and pneumonia, but some of the tests require lab cultures, and those take time. This is why I recommend we keep her here in the hospital until we get the test results back, which won't be until tomorrow, or the next day at the latest."

"I've already told Levy I'll stay with the baby," Jane told him. "He has farm animals to take care of."

"That's fine. We can provide a bed for you in the baby's room. Since the baby is familiar with you, she'll be calmer under your care anyway."

Levy looked at Jane. "I'll have to figure out some way to get home…"

"How did you get here?" inquired Dr. Forster. "Did you use a horse and buggy?"

"No, an *Englisch* friend drove us in."

"I can call a car to bring you home," offered the doctor.

"Thank you, I would appreciate that."

After the physician left to make arrangements, Levy dropped into a chair. "I'm trying not to think how much this will cost," he muttered.

Though medical costs were often shared by the community, Jane understood the reluctance to add to anyone's financial burden. "It's better to have a healthy baby," she told him. "It sounds like it could have been very, very serious if we hadn't brought her in."

"*Ja*, you're right. And *Gott* will provide us the way to pay for everything. But it also means I'll need to work harder at the farmer's market." He quirked a grim smile at her. "Those pints of raspberry jam will be very welcome in the booth."

"Well, I won't take any money for the ones that sell." Jane dropped down into the chair next to him. "It will all go toward the hospital costs."

He didn't argue.

A nurse emerged. "Mr. Struder, a car will be here in a few minutes to bring you home."

"Can I see Mercy?"

"Of course. But don't be alarmed by her appearance."

Jane's stomach clenched as she and Levy followed the nurse into the bowels of the hospital.

Stepping into Mercy's room, they saw her lying in a crib. Wires connected her to monitors. She was sleeping.

"She's tired out from the tests," said the nurse. "Sleeping is the best thing she can do right now. It'll help her heal."

"I hate seeing her here," Jane confessed.

"But she's improving. Unless she takes a turn for the worse, and we don't expect that to happen, we'll keep her on antibiotics for another twenty-four hours or so. By then we'll have some of the lab results back. If things look positive, we can release her while we wait for the rest of the cultures to come back." The nurse smiled. "I expect you'll be able to bring her home twenty-four hours from now, though she'll need some follow-up visits."

Levy nodded and Jane saw him swallow. "It scares

me to think what might have happened if we hadn't brought her in."

"Older babies can spike a fever of unknown origin, and while it's a little scary for the parents, it generally passes without a problem," said the nurse. "But in newborns, fevers can be life-threatening. We may not find out what caused it, but the critical thing is to either treat—or rule out—the very serious illnesses."

Levy reached out and gently cupped Mercy's head with his hand, and Jane saw his lips move in prayer. Then he stepped back. "I'd best get home. I have a lot of work to do." He looked at Jane. "I'll come back with the buggy tomorrow afternoon."

"*Ja.*" She watched as he turned and made his way out of the hospital room. "He's so worried," she murmured.

The nurse heard. "He's the uncle, right?"

"*Ja.* And part of his worry stems from not knowing where his sister is, the baby's mother."

The nurse's expression was sympathetic. "He seems like a good man."

"*Ja*, he is."

The nurse grew brisk. "I'm assuming you don't have a change of clothes, but we can give you a hospital gown to sleep in for the night, if you like. We also have a small library if you'd like something to read while you're here."

"Thank you."

The nurse showed Jane where the bookshelves were located, then departed for her duties. Jane chose a few books as well as a Bible, then returned to Mercy's room.

It seemed very strange to sit in a chair beside the

baby's crib, confined to a cheerful but serious hospital room full of unknown equipment.

With some relief, she heard Mercy stir and whimper, then the whimper turned into a thin fretful cry. A different nurse came hurrying in.

Jane felt helpless. "Is she okay?"

"Seems so." The nurse read various monitors over the crib. "Yes, I think she's just hungry. And wet."

"Can I change her? And feed her?"

"Of course. Holding her is about the best thing you can do right now, though you'll have to be careful of her IV tube and the wire connections."

The nurse provided a tiny disposable diaper, which Jane—used to cloth diapers—managed to fit onto the baby. The nurse showed her how to avoid tangling with the tubes and wires while she picked Mercy up and cradled her.

She sank down into the room's comfortable glider rocking chair while the nurse prepared a bottle of formula. Mercy was fretful until Jane slipped the tip into the baby's mouth. Immediately she started sucking.

"Ah, that's a good sign. She has an appetite," said the nurse. "Hold her as long as you like. She'll enjoy the body contact. I'll check up on you in a few minutes."

Jane leaned back, watching the infant's face as she nursed. Mercy's eyes stayed closed, and she seemed tired, but there was no question she was hungry. She nearly finished the bottle.

Jane flipped a hospital towel over her shoulder and lifted Mercy onto her shoulder, careful not to touch the IV tube and monitor wires, and patted her back until she burped. Then Jane slid Mercy down onto her chest and rocked as the baby relaxed into sleep.

Slow tears trickled down Jane's face as she realized how much Mercy had come to mean to her. She blessed her Aunt Catherine for encouraging them to take the baby to the hospital right away. What would have happened if she had kept her home, only to have her take a turn for the worse?

Now thanks be to *Gott*, this precious, vulnerable bundle was still alive and resting against her chest. Jane didn't want to let her go.

Exhausted, she dozed until the nurse came in. "Everything all right?"

Jane blinked. "*Ja*. She fell right asleep after her bottle. Should she go back to her crib or can I keep holding her?"

"Oh, hold her, by all means. Babies do best when they're held and loved." The nurse moved about the room, taking notes, straightening some items. "Can I bring you some dinner?"

"No, thank you, I already ate."

"Some tea, perhaps?"

"Oh, thank you. That would be wonderful."

So the nurse brought Jane a paper cup of steaming water and a little basket filled with tea bags and sugar packets, which she placed on a small sturdy table near the rocking chair. She helped prepare the tea, since Jane was unable to use both hands to make the tea herself. Then she brought the small pile of books Jane had borrowed and set them on the table as well.

"You look like you've done this before," Jane said, smiling.

"Yes, we often have parents staying with their sick babies. They usually don't want to do anything but hold them."

Jane rested her hand on Mercy's back. "I can understand why."

"But she's not your baby? You're the nanny?"

"*Ja*, but it's not hard to fall in love with something this precious."

The nurse smiled. "This baby is in good hands."

Left alone, Jane sipped her tea and managed to thumb open one of the books. Mercy breathed easily, and the horrible fever heat had left her body.

The words of the book blurred as Jane's thoughts wandered. It was true what she'd just admitted to the nurse: she had fallen in love with Mercy. She supposed it would be hard not to love the vulnerable motherless infant with such a sweet disposition.

Back in Jasper, as her friends started to get married and have families, Jane felt left behind. Her *Gott*-given gift to soothe babies had been appreciated by her friends whenever they'd needed an extra pair of hands, but Jane had never fallen in love with the babies she'd cared for. She'd never experienced motherly love and, after Isaac married Hannah, she wondered if she ever would.

Until now.

A slow tear leaked out of the corner of her eye. This baby wasn't hers. It wasn't even Levy's. It was Eliza's. If the mysteriously absent sister ever decided to return to Grand Creek, wouldn't she want her baby back?

Levy was another difficulty. Despite his prickly personality and touchiness over how he'd raised his sister, he was a good man…a fact not lost on Jane. She'd seen him at his worst, and his worst wasn't bad. She was trying hard not to fall in love with him. Levy saw her as a *useful* person, just as Isaac did. Not as a potential wife. Falling in love with him would be as painful as losing Isaac.

It seemed her new life here in Grand Creek was turning out to be just as complicated as her life in Jasper.

Chapter Ten

Jane ended up holding Mercy in her arms most of the night, dozing in the rocking chair and keeping the baby snuggled against her chest. A nurse came in every couple of hours to check on Mercy and examine the IV. She seemed pleased at the baby's progress. Jane changed the infant's diaper once and fed her twice during the night.

"A healthy appetite is a good sign," the night nurse assured her when she came in during her rounds and saw Jane feeding Mercy. "She looks like she's progressing well."

As the sun rose over the cars in the parking lot outside the hospital window, Jane laid the sleeping baby in her crib and stretched her cramped muscles. Heavy-eyed, she stumbled into the bathroom, removed her *kapp*, splashed water on her face, tidied her hair and made herself neat. Looking in the mirror, she winced at the dark circles under her eyes.

By the time the doctor came in on his morning rounds, Mercy was awake and quiet.

"Let's see how she's doing. She looks better," said Dr. Forster. He went to the baby in the crib and did a brief exam while Jane watched. The physician took Mercy's temperature, listened to her lungs, examined her eyes and mouth, and smiled.

"She's a fighter, this kid," he told the hovering Jane. "I think we can take her IV tube out, but I'd like to keep her on the monitors. We'll get some of the lab results back today, which will give us some indication what may have caused the fever. But if she continues improving and shows no more signs of fever throughout the day, I see no problem with discharging her this afternoon."

"That's a relief. I've been so worried." She closed her eyes and whispered a prayer of thanksgiving.

"You look like you were up all night with her." The doctor eyed her.

"*Ja*, I just dozed in the rocking chair but held her all night."

He smiled. "I wouldn't be surprised if that contributed to Mercy's improvement. Many people underestimate the importance of holding a baby as a factor in their healthy development. I see a lot of mothers who put their babies in cribs or strollers or playpens, but seldom hold them. Physical contact is especially important for babies who are bottle-fed."

"I use this a lot too." Jane rummaged in the diaper bag and plucked out the sling. "I can carry her around while doing chores."

"Excellent." Dr. Forster glanced at his watch. "You're

probably in for a boring day until Mercy is discharged this afternoon."

"I have books to read." Jane gestured toward the pile. "Do you have many Amish patients?"

"Of course. Since I'm a pediatrician, I treat many farm kids for injuries or illnesses." He smiled and then left Mercy's room to continue his rounds.

As predicted, it was indeed a boring day for Jane. Hours later, Dr. Forster came back, holding a file, just as the nurse poked her head in the door. "Dr. Forster? Mr. Struder is here, the baby's uncle. Did you want to talk to him?"

"Yes, can you bring him in?"

The nurse disappeared and reappeared a few minutes later with Levy. He was much cleaner than yesterday and wore a fresh shirt, though he also had circles under his eyes. Jane's heart jumped when he walked in.

Dr. Forster shook his hand. "Did you have a bad night's sleep?" he quipped.

"*Ja*, I kept imagining the worst." He peered at Mercy. "Is…is she better?"

"Much better, and I'll be discharging her shortly. However, I'd like some way to get hold of you in a hurry if the remaining lab results come back with anything alarming." He held up a hand. "I don't anticipate that happening, but I'll need some way to reach you. Do you have a neighbor with a phone?"

"*Ja*. They don't live next door, but they're not far away."

"Do you know their phone number?"

"No, but I can get it."

"Then here's my business card. That way if something comes up, you can reach me."

"*Ja*, sure." Levy slipped the card into a pocket.

"Now let's discuss follow-up care…"

He spent several minutes relating what additional symptoms to watch for, and urged Levy to bring the baby in for a follow-up appointment at the hospital's attached clinic the next week.

"I have a question," said Jane. "Levy sells produce at the farmer's market on Saturdays. It's helpful to have another person work the booth with him, so I bring Mercy and help when needed, though most of the time he's the one interacting with customers. Would it be all right to bring Mercy to the farmer's market by Saturday, or is it better for us to stay home?"

"Assuming she acts healthy and shows no signs of additional problems, I see no reason why you can't resume your normal activities," said the doctor. "However, I wouldn't let anyone else hold her."

Levy looked relieved. "Thank you. That will be a big help."

"Can she go outside?" persisted Jane. "The reason I ask is the nurse mentioned the fever probably didn't come from sunstroke, but I want to make sure I'm not making anything worse. Is it okay to bring her outside? I put her on a blanket in the shade. Otherwise I'll keep her in the house."

"No, by all means feel free to bring her outside. But yes, keep her fully in the shade, especially since it's been so hot lately."

"*Danke*."

The doctor smiled and shook both their hands. "Check out at the registration desk before you go, and we'll see you in a week."

Levy picked up the diaper bag. Jane slipped Mercy into the sling and walked out of the room that had seen such drama in the last twenty-four hours.

Leaning back in the buggy seat, Jane sighed as Levy clucked to the horse and guided her out of the hospital parking lot. "I'm glad that's over. I don't like hospitals."

"Neither do I. *Ach*, what a rotten night I had, not knowing what was going on. I can't imagine it was any better for you."

"Actually, it probably was. I didn't get much sleep, of course, but at least I knew what was going on." Jane peered at Mercy, snug against her chest in the sling. "Remind me to thank the *Englisch* neighbor who drove us in yesterday. I was so distracted I didn't even catch his name."

"Well, we have to talk to him anyway to ask him to leave his phone number with the hospital, so that would be a good time."

"I'll bring him baked goods or jam in thanks."

"Just so you know, I let your aunt and uncle know you were at the hospital last night."

"*Danke*! I forgot all about them. I'm glad you let them know." She fell silent a moment and watched the town transition from city streets to rural roads. "So how far behind did you fall on the farm work?"

"It's going to be a challenge to have enough for Saturday's farmer's market," he admitted. "Between the rain and the hospital, a lot of this week was shot. I'm trying not to worry about money."

"What can I do to help?" she said. "I can't leave Mercy alone in the house, of course, and I don't want to expose her to full sunshine after what happened, but is there anything I can do to be—" she paused over her word choice "—useful?"

"The raspberry jam will be a huge help. If you can continue picking raspberries and turning them into jam, that would be wonderful. Whatever jam doesn't sell can be held until the following week, since it won't go bad. But with the amount of raspberries coming in at the moment, it's the only way to use them up. I'll pick some for selling fresh on Friday."

"*Ja*, I'll keep making raspberry jam then. But I'll make sure to pick them earlier in the day before it gets terribly hot."

Levy sighed, then asked Jane, "What about this evening? You've been on duty nonstop for thirty-six hours with the baby at the hospital. Should I take you straight home?"

Every instinct cried out for rest, but Jane knew Levy was already overstressed, and she wouldn't feel right going home while he watched Mercy. "I have an idea," she offered. "Let's go by your place first and let me pick up that portable crib and some other things for the baby, then take us both to my aunt and uncle's. She can spend the night with me. That way my aunt can fuss over her while I get cleaned up, and I'll be able to keep an eye on her all night."

"*Ja*, that would be great." Levy spoke with obvious relief. "*Danke*."

Half an hour later, having picked up what she needed for the baby, Levy pulled the horse to a stop in front of the Troyers' home. Her aunt popped out of the house. "You're here!"

"*Guder nammidaag*, Tante Catherine." Jane gave Mercy to Levy while she climbed out of the buggy, then took the child while he hopped down and unloaded the baby supplies. "I'm going to keep Mercy here for the night, if that's all right with you."

"*Ja*! Of course! Here, I'll take the *boppli*." She took the child into her experienced arms and started cooing at the tiny alert face.

"I'll be over tomorrow around seven in the morning," Jane told Levy. "That way I can start picking raspberries before it gets too hot."

"*Ja, danke. Vielen Dank* for everything." He gave her a long look, filled with something Jane didn't understand, then clucked to the horse and started down the road.

She stared after him for a moment, then turned to her aunt.

Catherine looked at Jane hard. "Seems like you've been awake all night. Am I right?"

"Close to it, *ja*." She punctuated this by a huge yawn. "I didn't even sleep in a bed, but held Mercy all night in a rocking chair."

Her aunt nodded with the wisdom of experience. "I've done that, though never in a hospital room. Come inside. I know your uncle wants to hear everything that happened."

Over dinner, with Mercy secure in her bouncy seat on the table, Jane related the last twenty-four hours. "With Mercy's hospitalization and his primary source of income at the moment coming from the farmer's market, he's stressed about money."

"It's up to Levy to figure out his finances," Peter said firmly.

"Your uncle is right." Catherine took a bite and spoke with her mouth full. "If Levy's going to keep this little *boppli*, he's going to have to figure out how to juggle all his commitments."

Her aunt paused for a moment, then continued. "I wonder if he's waiting for Eliza to come back?" she mused. "I mean, clearly he's nurturing some sort of hope for his sister's redemption."

"That young woman who didn't see the need to be baptized," growled Uncle Peter with uncharacteristic hostility. "She could have married Josiah Lapp, who's a fine *youngie*, but instead she left Grand Creek for the *Englisch* world and now Josiah is interested in the Miller girl."

Jane's ears pricked up. "Did this Josiah Lapp lead her on or anything?"

"*Nein*, just the opposite. Eliza was something of a flirt, but Josiah was stuck on her something fierce. When she left, it took him a while to get over it."

Perhaps Jane's sympathies should lie more with Josiah than with Eliza, since she too had been jilted by the person she loved. Well, she could hardly call it *jilted* if

Isaac had never realized she was in love with him. Still, she felt a stirring interest in Eliza's fate.

"Well, whatever happened, she had a beautiful baby." Jane touched Mercy, and the infant immediately clasped her finger with a tiny hand. "She's such a joy to take care of. When she's not spiking a fever, that is."

Catherine chuckled. "You always had a gift for babies. Maybe someday…"

For once Jane didn't feel the familiar stab of pain. "Maybe someday I'll get married and have some of my own?"

"I'm sorry, child, I shouldn't have said that."

"Don't worry. You reminded me what I'd forgotten for a bit, that I should turn my future over to *Gott*. I'm willing to wait and see what He has in store for me," Jane said, then added, "And that's the first time I've felt optimistic about it too."

"*Gott* works in mysterious ways," Peter told her. "And who knows, maybe He'll restore Eliza back to the community, in which case she can raise her own baby."

Jane thought about the mysterious Eliza as she prepared for bed. She settled Mercy into her portable crib and slid between the sheets, watching the baby, grateful she seemed fully recuperated from her illness.

How would she feel if Eliza suddenly returned and claimed the baby as her own? She had every right to raise her own child, but Jane knew it would be a difficult thing to stop caring for this infant who had come to mean so much to her.

Along with Levy.

Jane rolled over and stared at the dark ceiling. Crickets chirped outside her open window, and she heard the hoot of an owl from a distance. She blasted herself for falling in love with another man like Isaac, who only saw her as "useful."

What was the matter with her that she could be "useful" but not lovable?

Chapter Eleven

Uncle Peter drove her and Mercy to Levy's farm the next morning, since Jane couldn't walk there while carrying the baby equipment and the baby.

"*Danke*," she told her uncle as he unloaded the portable crib, diaper bag and bouncy seat on Levy's front porch. "I'll be home this afternoon."

Levy wasn't in the house. Jane walked through the quiet home, noting dirty dishes in the sink and a small pile of laundry on the floor. She smiled despite herself at his clear lack of domestic skills.

Before doing anything else, though, she carried buckets, a blanket and the baby outside to harvest raspberries before the day got too hot. She settled Mercy in the shade and began picking.

By the time Levy returned from the fields, the sun was high and her buckets were full. Mercy's diaper needed changing, and the baby began making noises indicating she was about to go into a full-fledged crying jag until her belly was filled.

"Here, I'll take the berries," offered Levy. "You take care of Mercy."

"*Ja, danke*, she's hungry and wet." Jane picked up the baby and returned to the house. She changed her diaper and settled into a rocking chair with a bottle of formula.

"No problems?" Levy settled onto a chair near the rocker as the baby nursed.

"*Nein*, she slept all night. Whatever caused the fever, it doesn't seem to be causing any additional problems."

He sighed with a relief Jane fully understood. "I'm grateful to *Gott* it wasn't worse. I don't know what I'd have said to Eliza if something happened to Mercy."

"And you have no possible way to get in touch with your sister? No address?"

"No." He stood up and returned to the kitchen. "I'm going to make myself a sandwich and get back outside. I have a lot to do to get ready for the farmer's market."

"I'll make jam this afternoon."

"*Ja, danke*."

Within a few minutes, he was gone and the house fell silent.

When Mercy fell asleep after her bottle, Jane laid the baby in her crib and commenced a quick housecleaning, ending with hanging laundry on the line. Then she started to make the raspberry jam.

Levy was grateful Jane arrived a bit earlier than normal on Saturday morning. "I've got your jars of raspberry jam already packed," he told her. "If you can take care of the baby, I'll finish loading the wagon."

"*Ja*, let me have her." He handed Mercy into her capable arms, and Jane slipped the infant into the sling.

"I've got a few more crates to pack, then we can be on our way," he added.

"What can I do?"

"I don't have Mercy's diaper bag or the lunch hamper packed. Can you work on those?"

"*Ja*, sure." She disappeared into the kitchen. He paused for a moment to admire her figure in the tidy green dress, then continued loading crates of lettuce and early carrots, flats of raspberries, fresh corn and tomatoes. In plenty of time, he was able to get the wagon on the road.

"Mercy seems fully recuperated." Levy guided the horse through an intersection. "But the back of the booth is well-shaded, and you might want to keep Mercy there rather than expose her to the crowds."

"*Ja*," agreed Jane. "I don't want her to pick up any germs."

"She's fortunate you're here to care for her." Levy kept his eyes on the horse's ears. The compliment fell clumsily from his lips. He covered the awkward moment by adding, "Still, I think I'm going to ask you to conduct a small experiment whenever Mercy is napping. How would you like to act as a scout?"

"A scout?" She glanced at him. "What do you mean?"

"I mean someone who can walk around the market. I'm always so busy at the booth that I seldom get to see what other people are selling."

"Are you thinking in terms of adding to your booth's inventory?"

"*Ja*, something like that." Finances had been on his mind a lot. "I have the hospital bills to pay off, so I want to learn what other things besides produce sell. Your jam is selling so well that I'm thinking it's time to go beyond just fruits and vegetables."

Jane chuckled. "So you want me to be an undercover spy."

He smiled. "Exactly."

"I'd be happy to. I'll wait until the crowds are thickest, and I'll see what people are buying the most of."

"*Danke.*"

The next few hours were busy. Following the unspoken pattern from the last few weekends, he set up the booth while Jane unloaded crates of produce. Once the booth was assembled, she joined him in stocking the display units.

"Here, you might like this." He held up a hand-lettered sign. "I made it last night."

"'Fresh Homemade Raspberry Jam,'" Jane read out loud. "'Meet the Expert Jam-Maker in Person.'" Her eyes crinkled in amusement. "Do you think it will help?"

"Can't hurt." He grinned and hung the sign over the jars of ruby-red jam.

Then, as customers started trickling and then flooding the market, he switched on his consummate salesman personality.

"It's like you become a whole different man," Jane said to him during a lull.

"What do you mean?"

"When customers come into the booth, it's like you

flip a switch. You're teasing and talkative, but without being obnoxious or pushy."

So she'd noticed. Levy couldn't help but be pleased. "Do you wish I could stay that way all the time?"

"No. It's effective while selling something, but it's not who you are. I… I like the other man better. The real you." She looked away, her cheeks turning pink.

A group of customers entered the booth and distracted him. He began to talk with them, while thinking about Jane's shy blush. He found he liked the idea of making her blush.

Jane stayed in the back of the booth, keeping Mercy in her sling unless she had to feed or diaper her, and watched as fruits and vegetables disappeared with magical speed. Levy had to constantly restock his inventory.

She hadn't meant to reveal that she liked the real Levy. The words just came out. She was glad when some customers had distracted him. Least said, soonest mended, as her mother always observed.

At a time when Mercy was sleeping in her basket and the crowds were at their heaviest, Levy gave her a nod and she slipped out of the booth. She avoided the Amish booths because she knew they sold similar items, but she was curious about the *Englisch* booths.

It was an eye-opener. Creative entrepreneurs sold everything from baked goods to soaps to knitted items to crafts, even gourmet dog biscuits.

Several items caught her eye as something Levy could do. She saw gift baskets packed with edible goodies, both fresh and baked, which sold briskly.

And eggs. Why wasn't Levy selling eggs? She saw cartons of farm-fresh eggs in nearly every bag a customer carried.

And potted plants. Jane saw a booth selling potted herbs that was busy with customers.

And baked goods. Cookies, breads, rolls, muffins, cupcakes and other items sold well.

And cut flowers. Women bought them in bulk.

And packages of dried herbs. Jane knew Levy grew some herbs, but he didn't sell any. Why not?

And dried glass gem corn. Jane knew this variety grew well in Indiana. People seemed to like it for decorative purposes. Levy didn't have any growing, but perhaps next year…

Her mind buzzed with the potential of how Levy could expand his sales. If he had hospital bills to pay off, he could put a lot more items up for sale and earn more money.

She returned to the booth in time to help him handle another surge of customers. "Yes, those are $2.99 a pound," she told a lady, slipping behind the table. She paused to check on Mercy, who slept soundly in her carrier basket, and turned back to the customer.

To her surprise, his signage drawing attention to the "Expert Jam-Maker" had garnered much more attention than she'd anticipated. Many people, mostly *Englisch* women, asked her how she made it. Jane was floored. Who didn't know how to make raspberry jam?

But she explained the steps to dozens of women as well as a few men over the course of the day. And the jars of jam disappeared until there were only two left.

And those final jars were snapped up by a grand-motherly woman late in the afternoon. She exclaimed over the jam and told Levy how much she used to enjoy making preserves with her mother and grandmother.

"Come back in a couple of weeks when the blueber-ries are ripe," Levy told her. "Jane makes blueberry jam that simply melts in your mouth."

"I will!" The woman tucked the jam into a canvas bag. "I don't do a lot of canning anymore, so I'll look forward to it."

After the happy customer departed, Jane eyed Levy. "You've never tasted my blueberry jam."

"*Nein*, but can you tell me it won't be anything but delicious?"

She laughed. "Well, I have to admit your sign worked. You sold seventy-five jars of jam!"

For the rest of the afternoon, sales were brisk and Levy seemed pleased as one item after another sold out. As was his usual custom, Levy was the last booth to break down at the end of the day, and he netted two extra sales as a result.

"Whew." With the wagon packed and the horse hitched up, Levy slumped as he directed the animal to-ward home. "This is why I look forward to the Sabbath. I'm always so tired by the end of farmer's market day."

"And I'm about to make you even more tired."

"What do you mean? Are you talking about your scouting expedition this afternoon?"

"*Ja.* There are many things you shouldn't even think about selling. A lot of vendors do, as you put it, 'the buy-and-sell.' Obviously there are no oranges grown in Indiana," she joked.

He chuckled. "*Ja*, I hope the vendors aren't trying to pass those off as what they grew themselves."

"And several booths sold things like crafts and homemade soaps. I assume you're not interested in competing."

"No. I don't have the time or the interest."

"But there were a lot of things you might consider. Eggs, for example. Why aren't you selling eggs?"

He looked bewildered. "Everyone sells eggs."

"And everyone sells out. Bring what eggs you have. Trust me, they'll sell."

He rubbed his chin. "I'll have to get cartons. They sell empty cartons at the feed store in town. What else did you see?"

"A few things you might think about for next year, but too late for this year. For example, you've seen glass gem corn, right?"

"*Ja*."

"One booth had ears for sale, and the vendor was selling lots of them. The *Englisch* like to use them for decoration."

"Hmm." He looked thoughtful. "It would be easy to plant that next summer, though I'll have to check the pollination timing. I can't have it crossing with my sweet corn. What else?"

"Flowers."

"Flowers?"

"*Ja*, cut flowers. Zinnias, daisies, black-eyed Susans, sunflowers, sweet peas, that kind of thing. All the *Englisch* women were buying them by the armfuls. Of course, that's more for next year too, but it's something to think about."

"*Gut, gut*. I can plan for next year. But what about this year?"

"Herbs. People are crazy for herbs. I notice you have some in the garden, so you might pot some cuttings and sell those. Rosemary, sage, thyme, parsley, mint, basil. It's a little late in the season, but I'll bet they'll sell. And dried herbs as well. I saw a lot of demand for dried herbs."

He nodded. "That wouldn't be hard to do."

"And baked goods. I saw people selling bread, cookies, cupcakes, rolls, muffins, cinnamon rolls, all kinds of things."

He shook his head. "That's not something I can do. I'm no good at baking."

"But I am."

He glanced at her. "You're doing enough, Jane. Not only are you taking care of Mercy, but you're doing the housework and making jam."

"*Ja*, sure, but you've got some hospital bills to pay off. Right now I think we both need to do as much as possible to sell things and pay off those bills. You don't want to make Mercy's hospital stay a burden to the rest of the community unless it's absolutely necessary."

He looked troubled. "I know. You're right. But it's a lot of extra work."

"Of course it is. But what we need to do is sit down and plan out each day's work. I can establish a baking schedule and make things to sell. Same with the jam.

You can add dried or potted herbs to your schedule as well as picking fruit for me to make into jam."

"That sounds *gut*. I wonder too—would your aunt and uncle like to send some of their dry-goods inventory over and we can sell some of those for a small commission?"

"You know what might work better? How about if we start looking at some of the things women in the church make already—dolls or small quilts or other sewn goods? You could buy them wholesale and sell them at your booth."

"*Ja*." He gave a dry chuckle. "I just bought this new booth. But I have a feeling I'm going to have to get a bigger one."

"What about your old booth? Is it still usable?"

"*Ja*, but it's too small."

"But can you add it to your new booth?"

"Hmmm." His brow furrowed. "Not to the side— the spaces on either side of me are rented. But maybe I can go deep. I could connect both booths into a deeper space. Fresh produce and baked goods could be up front, and dry goods and other things like that could go farther in." He looked out into the distance, and Jane could almost see the gears in his brain churning. "I'd have to make new signage inviting customers to walk all the way to the back, but it would open up a lot more display space…"

"We'll make this work, Levy."

He sighed. "I've never had a partner before. Always, I've been on my own."

She was startled. "I'm not your partner, Levy. I'm just Mercy's nanny."

He went silent. She worked so well with him, sometimes she suspected he forgot.

And, if she were truly honest with herself, so did she.

Jane set herself daily tasks toward providing more products to sell at the market. Levy busied himself with combining his old and new booths into one larger booth.

"Come see what you think!" he called into the house on a Wednesday afternoon.

Jane picked up the baby and walked out to where he had set the booths up near the barn. "*Ach*, it looks *gut*!" she exclaimed.

He had reconfigured the two structures to allow display racks down the length of both sides, with a small area in back where non-sale items such as chairs, the diaper bag and other personal things could be stored behind a screen. The booth was now ten feet wide and twenty feet deep.

"See, these curtains will hide the unsold produce." He lifted a length of cheerful red gingham skirts tacked across the bottoms of the displays. "I can stack crates of fruits and vegetables under here, and they'll stay cool and shaded and out of sight. But everything will be easy to restock. The sales table and scale will be here. Your jams can be displayed there. These shelves above will be for potted herbs. Next year if I have more to sell, such as cut flowers or decorative corn, I can add bins to this area." He pointed. "And I'll put up signs here and here with arrows pointing inward, so people know they can walk all the way to the back."

"It looks *wunnerschee*," enthused Jane. "It will make a huge difference in your sales, Levy, I'm sure of it."

"I can't wait to try it out this Saturday." Levy looked up at the slatted roof topped with burlap, which offered shade but allowed breezes to flow through. "I think it will work."

"By the way, don't forget Mercy has a follow-up appointment with the doctor this afternoon."

He groaned. "I forgot." He took off his hat and scratched his head in frustration. "And I have a lot to do." He thought for a moment, then said, "Are you comfortable driving yourself to the doctor? Maggie the horse, she's well trained and easy to handle."

"*Ja*, sure, I've driven a buggy a fair bit. I'll take her in myself."

Jane gave herself plenty of time to get to the hospital for Mercy's checkup. Levy was right: the horse was easy to guide. In the hospital parking lot, she hitched Maggie under the shade of a large tree at a rail set up for the town's Amish population. She slipped Mercy into the sling, took the diaper bag and went into the hospital.

Dr. Forster was delighted to see the baby. "You'll be happy to know all the tests came back negative," he told her as he laid the infant on a padded table and examined her. "We may never know what spiked that fever, but I can't tell you how glad I am to see her looking so healthy. No more issues?"

"No. None." Jane related the week's events.

The doctor picked up the infant and cuddled her for

a moment, then handed her to Jane. "This baby is lucky to have you caring for her, Miss Troyer. Keep on doing the excellent job you're doing."

"Thank you, Doctor." Jane slipped the baby into the sling. Then she shook the doctor's hand and made her way out of the hospital.

In the midst of processing the fruit for jam the next day, Jane heard a knock at the door. She wiped away sweat from her forehead with her sleeve and felt a moment's annoyance. She didn't look her best and she was in the middle of a messy project. The propane cookstove was laden with large pots of water heating toward a boil, and one huge pot in which she was stirring crushed berries. She sighed, washed her hands and went to answer the door.

"*Guder nammidaag*!" sang her friends Sarah and Rhoda when Jane opened the door. "We've brought company!"

"Come in, come in!" Jane spoke with cheer, but her heart sank when she saw the other visitor was Charles, the young man who had paid her such attention at the singing. "I'm in the middle of canning jam, so let's visit in the kitchen."

Jane was able to conjure up a plate of cookies. The baby woke up, and soon enough she was being passed around by the young women. Little Mercy smiled with all the attention.

Charles didn't say much, but his eyes followed Jane's every move as she stirred the mashed raspberries on the propane stove and added the sugar and lemon juice. Jane was conscious of his interest, his scrutiny, his flattering attention. Yet after all she'd been through with Mercy in the hospital and then ramping up making items to sell at the farmer's market, he seemed to pale in comparison to Levy's constant industry and hardheaded common sense.

"We haven't seen you for the last few days," Rhoda said.

"It's been so busy here. It's the height of the berry season and work has been nonstop."

"Where's Levy now?" asked Sarah.

"Berry picking," Jane replied. "He's getting the last of the raspberries, but their season is mostly over. Now the blueberries are starting to peak, and he has a lot of blueberry bushes. He's also selling a lot of the fruit fresh. You know Mercy had to spend a night in the hospital, *ja*? It put Levy behind schedule, so we've both been working twice as hard to make things to sell at the farmer's market."

"Do you go too?" inquired Charles. "To the farmer's market, that is?"

"*Ja.*" Jane smiled at the young man. He was nice-looking but seemed boyish in comparison to Levy. "I don't really do any of the selling, but it's helpful to have another pair of hands. And do you know what Levy did?" She gestured toward the kettle of boiling fruit. "He made a sign saying 'Meet the Expert Jam-Maker in Person!' that he hangs when he puts the jam out for sale. I've learned a lot of *Englisch* don't make their own jam, and I get so many people asking questions."

Sarah and Rhoda chuckled at the story. But Charles,

she noted, had to force his smile. She nodded to herself. *Gut*. He understood the subtle innuendo and unspoken nuance of the tale, and picked up the message that she, Jane, was tied up with Levy's business plans and therefore not available as a romantic interest. She felt a little bad, but she didn't want him harboring any thoughts she wasn't interested in sharing.

Besides, there were lots of other girls in the *youngie* group. Prettier girls. Jane knew she only stood out because she was new in the community, but she had no illusion about her looks and knew Charles could get any number of other young women to return his affection.

The pot on the stove boiled, and Jane stirred in the rest of the sugar and kept stirring for about a minute before she removed the pot from the heat and skimmed off the foam. She set out the pint jars she'd sterilized earlier and began filling them with a wide-mouth funnel while the group chattered behind her.

"Ah, that's the hardest part of the jam done." She wiped sweat from her forehead and lifted the lid off the pots of water to check the temperature. She capped the jam and lifted the jars into the pots.

"How many pints of jam do you hope to make?" inquired Sarah.

"As many as we have raspberries for," Jane replied. She replaced the lids on the pots and dropped onto a kitchen chair with a sigh. "I'll repeat this process tomorrow with whatever berries have ripened. *Ach*, I'm tired. It's such a busy season for Levy, and now I understand why."

"I suppose we should leave you to your work then." Rhoda finished eating the last of her cookie.

"I'm glad you visited." Jane spoke the truth. She liked Sarah and Rhoda, and it was good to clear the air with Charles. "I don't know how many *youngie* events I'll be able to attend for the rest of the summer since it's so busy here, but I'm sure that will change after the harvest season is over."

"*Ja*, we'll let you know what's planned. We'll see you on Church Sunday."

Jane saw her friends out the door, then returned to the kitchen. Little Mercy began making hunger noises, so Jane prepared a bottle, checked the status of the jam and took the baby into the other room so she could settle into the rocking chair while she fed her.

She rocked and smiled. She realized the visit from the three people cheered her up. They hadn't forgotten her. And Charles—well, he was a nice young man. He would have no trouble finding someone to court.

It just wasn't going to be her.

"This new booth arrangement is working better than I'd hoped," Levy murmured to Jane on Saturday, as he watched the crowd. "Sales are better than ever."

Jane scanned the customers. "Everyone seems to like it."

Levy watched the play of dappled sunshine on Jane's face and realized how much he enjoyed working with her. Her industriousness—especially while caring for an infant—staggered him. And her help during these busy summer months was yielding astounding results.

He realized she had a head for business that exceeded his own. She was smart, savvy and intuitive.

He listened as customers expressed appreciation for the new booth layout. "You can thank her," he often said, waving a hand toward Jane. "She's the genius behind the design."

The first time he said that, he saw the glow of appreciation on her face. For a moment he was poleaxed and realized how very pretty she was. It was something he had no time to dwell on, because of how quickly customers bought things. Every pot of herbs sold. So did every jar of jam and every last baked good Jane had made. He sold out of corn, beans, peas, raspberries, blueberries, tomatoes and almost all the other produce.

At the end of the day, after the wagon was packed, Levy clucked to the horse to start for home. "I don't think I've ever had such *gut* sales."

"We need to ride this wave." Jane gently bounced Mercy in her lap. "If you keep this up, the hospital bills will be paid in no time."

"Rebecca Yoder said she had some fabric items she'd be interested in selling. A few dolls, a couple of baby quilts, that kind of thing."

"And my friend Sarah has some small rag rugs she said we could display."

"The raspberries are about done, but the blueberries are starting to peak. Are you up for making blueberry jam?"

"Of course."

He smiled. "I don't know how I would manage without you, Jane. *Vielen Dank* for all your help."

"This is fun. A lot of work, *ja*, but it's a direct connection—providing what people want."

She lapsed into silence, holding the baby close while she watched the passing town. Levy snuck looks at her, wondering why on earth she ever thought herself plain. There was a sparkle to her, an animation he admired. Yet she also had a soothing presence, a calming influence.

He remembered her uncertainty about how long she planned to stay in Grand Creek. He realized how much he was depending on her—not just as Mercy's nanny, but for her assistance at the farmer's market, for her business instincts, for her industriousness. And maybe, just maybe, for herself.

"Jane," he said, "I know you said you didn't know how long you would stay in town. Is it possible for you to stay until after the farmer's market season is over?"

She turned toward him, her blue eyes bright behind her glasses. "When does the market end for the season?"

"The last weekend in October."

"That's three months off."

"*Ja*. Were you planning on leaving sooner?" His heart sped up as he waited for her answer.

"I don't know." She spoke thoughtfully. "I miss my family, of course, but I can see why you'd need me to stay until the season is over. Let me think on it."

"*Ja, danke*." He knew he couldn't push, but he also knew he wanted her to stay.

For a long time.

Chapter Twelve

"She's really starting to hold her head up now. Look at that." Jane pointed.

It was late September. Mercy lay on a blanket on her stomach under the shade of the maple tree. As Levy walked up, sweaty and dirty from a day in the fields, she raised her head and smiled at him.

He sat down on the grass to rest for a moment. "What a little beauty."

"Nearly three months old already." Jane dangled a small toy before the infant. "It seems like July was just yesterday, when I started taking care of her. She's growing so fast."

He looked out at the verdant garden and fields as the sun dropped lower in the sky. "I wonder if Eliza ever wonders about Mercy and how she is."

"Every single day, I would imagine."

He stayed silent a few moments, gazing to the west. "The pumpkins are starting to turn orange," he commented at last. "I think a few might be ripe enough to bring to the farmer's market this Saturday."

"You seem tired." Jane also thought he looked distracted and moody, but it would have been rude to mention it.

He sighed. "I am. Since I combined the booths a couple months ago, sometimes it's hard to keep up with the increased sales. Still, I'm grateful to *Gott* for everything. This summer has been the most profitable it's ever been. I've been able to pay every bill to the hospital myself so far, without having to ask the community to help."

Jane knew that was a huge motivating factor behind his hard work. He had no wish for his sister's baby to be a financial burden on his church family.

"Well, only four more weeks to get through." Jane's voice wavered for a brief moment. In four weeks—in theory—Levy would no longer need her help in nannying Mercy. Their work schedule throughout the summer had meshed so seamlessly that it was hard to imagine not seeing him on a daily basis. The very thought made her heart lurch in her chest.

She thought she'd learned her lesson back home in Ohio. Why did it seem she was destined to fall in love with men who didn't see her as a woman? Levy, she knew, appreciated her help in everything from Mercy's care to the items she made to sell. He was, by every indicator, an excellent boss.

It wasn't his fault she had fallen in love with him.

But she kept her emotions in check. She'd grown up

a lot over the summer and refused to become the love-lorn figure she was when she first arrived. Besides, Levy had given no indication he returned her affections, and she wasn't about to make a fool of herself. Again.

She forced her mind back to the present. "I'm going to start making peach chutney this week," she said. "The peaches are beautiful. All your fruit trees are doing well."

He gave a small groan as he rose to his feet. "*Ach*, my sore muscles. There are some crates of peaches in the basement, ripening," he added. "Go ahead and use those."

She watched as he went back to work. That was another thing she'd come to admire over the last two months. His work ethic. He never seemed to stop. She didn't think she'd ever met a man as hardworking as Levy.

By the time Saturday rolled around, Jane had pulled together fifty pints of peach chutney, two dozen pints of applesauce, two dozen pints of tomato salsa and three dozen quarts of apple pie filling.

In addition to the full bounty of a September harvest, Levy had expanded into offering packets of seeds for customers to purchase. He made brown-paper envelopes, and on each envelope he wrote out the types of seeds and basic planting directions. Jane used a tiny green ribbon to close the flaps.

The booth, when it was set up at the Saturday market, was packed to capacity with goods for sale.

"There." Levy finished tying some corn stalks for decoration at the booth corners before the market opened. He took off his hat and wiped a hand across his brow. "Let's pray sales are *gut* today."

By the time they were ready to break down in the late afternoon, nearly everything had sold. The packets of seeds were especially popular, another component that surprised him. "Unbelievable," he muttered to Jane. "Seeds are available everywhere. Why would people buy so many here?"

She picked up the one remaining unsold packet. "These look *gut*. And people know the seeds come from your farm. I've come to realize how many people like knowing the sources for things."

"I've never had a summer like this." He started breaking down the booth components so they could be loaded into the wagon. "*Ach*, I'm glad tomorrow is the Sabbath."

"*Ja*, it will be good to rest."

Jane helped him load the boxes and crates, and the wagon started for home.

Jane thought Levy still seemed distracted, almost nervous. "I'll throw together a quick dinner before I go home tonight," she offered.

"*Danke*," he answered, then fell silent.

She didn't know what to make of his behavior. He didn't seem angry. She'd had no cross words with him in weeks. They seemed to work well together. What could possibly be wrong?

When he pulled up to the house, Jane took Mercy inside and started dinner while Levy groomed and fed Maggie and put the booth away for the week. By the time he came inside, she had the table set.

Levy sluiced his face at the sink as Jane pulled food from the oven. He sat down at the table and fidgeted. He shuffled. He fretted.

"Levy, are you *oll recht*?" she asked after they'd said grace. "You seem as nervous as a cat." She poured herself some milk.

"*Ja*, sure." He took a bite, then laid his fork down. "Jane, I have a question for you."

"*Ja*? What is it?"

"Would you consider marrying me?"

Jane couldn't believe what she was hearing. "What? Did I hear you right?"

"Yes."

"Levy, where did this come from?"

"I think it's a logical question. You're so good with Mercy. You're amazing in everything you do…"

Jane's temper rose. If she had ever entertained any hopes about her and Levy, they were dashed on the rocks at the bottom of her heart. There was no mention of love, of warmth or affection or anything else upon which a stable long-term marriage could be built.

Her answer was short. "No."

He winced. "I'm sorry I asked so bluntly, please won't you reconsider…"

"Levy, do you expect me to marry someone who only sees me as a baby nurse?" She got to her feet so fast the chair went flying and crashed to the floor. Mercy whimpered.

He looked surprised. "Just a baby nurse? Jane, hasn't it been obvious that my feelings for you have grown over the summer?"

She stared as her heart continued to pound in thick, painful thuds. "No. It *hasn't* been obvious."

"I thought we were getting along so well…"

"Sure, as an employer and employee. Not as a husband and wife."

He, too, rose to his feet. "Then I've been remiss. I've… I've never courted before. This is new territory for me."

For Levy to admit such a weakness drained Jane's anger. But the tiny portion of her heart that longed for romance shrank from him. Her mind flip-flopped this way and that, trying to come to terms with this new development.

"Besides," he added, "I can't take care of the baby on my own."

Her heart sank. *Useful* again. Never romantic.

And yet…and yet…was that really such a bad thing? She loved him, and even if he didn't return her feelings, they got along well and had the baby to unite them. Could such a marriage work?

"That's what the bishop is urging you to do, ain't so?" she asked. "Marry?"

"*Ja*. If you marry me, we can raise Mercy together." He raised an eyebrow. "That's the most logical, rational solution to the problem."

She lifted her chin. "If you want a logical, rational answer, then here's mine. I can't help but feel this proposal springs from guilt. I think your guilt over what happened to your sister is coloring your views on what's important to the baby. You insist on keeping Mercy rather than letting her be raised by a family…"

"But I *am* her family!"

"*Nein*, you're her uncle who has a living to make and can't take care of an infant on your own. You're doing the best you can, but it's impossible to care for the needs of a baby while you work a farm."

"But wouldn't marrying me solve that problem?"

"Marriage is permanent. It's a lifelong commitment. There would be no going back. That's a lot to ask of me."

"Jane." Levy placed a hand on her arm, and his voice was gentle. "Are you saying you have no feelings for me?"

She stared at his hand and her throat thickened. "I… I don't know," she stammered. "All I know is men don't look at me twice because I'm plain. To suddenly believe you want to marry me for anything else besides a built-in nanny is hard for me to comprehend." Tears welled up in her eyes.

He tipped her chin up so her eyes met his. "You keep thinking you're plain, and I don't understand why. You've never been plain to me."

Coming from any other man, Jane wouldn't have believed that statement. But with Levy…well, it was possible he spoke truly. She knew she had fostered respect from him through the summer. Could it have grown into something more?

She stepped back and broke contact, though her skin tingled where he had touched her. "Levy, this is so sudden. I can't give you an answer yet."

"Then think about it. Tomorrow is the Sabbath. Let *Gott* guide your thinking, and we can talk on Monday."

"*Ja. Gut.*" She backed up another step, suddenly desperate to get away. "Then I'll leave Mercy to you. *Gude nacht*, Levy." She turned and fled.

Her footsteps pounded in her ears as she walked home. She felt a need to talk things over with her aunt. She needed the calm, levelheaded advice of the older woman to get over this hurdle.

Walking into her aunt and uncle's house, she found them sitting in the living room with newspapers. "Tante Catherine, can I talk to you?" Her voice sounded strained even to her own ears.

Her relatives raised their heads. Uncle Peter looked at her face and rose from his chair. "I just remembered I have some work that needs doing in the barn." He left the room. Jane made a mental note to thank him later.

"You're white as a sheet," observed Catherine. "Sit down, child, and tell me what happened."

Jane sat down and promptly burst into tears.

Catherine handed her a handkerchief and stayed quiet while Jane continued to cry.

"Tell me what happened, *liebling*," she said after the storm had passed and Jane wiped her cheeks dry.

"Levy asked me to marry him," Jane blurted out.

Catherine's eyebrows shot up into her hairline. "What!"

"That was pretty much my reaction. Essentially he wants a built-in nanny-housekeeper for Mercy, and this was the most logical, rational solution he could think of."

"Did this happen just out of the blue?"

"*Ja.*" Jane toyed with the handkerchief. "And...and I don't know what to do. I don't understand why he thought I would agree to a one-sided marriage..."

Catherine snapped her head up. "One-sided?"

Jane fell silent.

"One-sided?" persisted her aunt. "What do you mean, one-sided?"

Jane heaved a shuddering sigh. "Just what I said. I've fallen in love with Levy—and the baby as well—but I don't know that I want to accept a marriage proposal when he doesn't return the sentiment."

"Oh *Schätzchen*. No wonder you're so upset. Here he could be offering you the moon and the stars, if only the sentiment was behind them."

"*Ja.* Exactly. Oh, Tante, what should I do?" The tears started again. "To Levy, I'm just another 'useful' person, just like I was with Isaac. Why don't men see me as a woman? Why am I always nothing more than a tool?"

"Are you sure he has no feelings for you? Levy's aware of the commitment behind a marriage. Surely he wouldn't propose if he didn't feel some affection for you?"

"He says he does, but I don't know that I believe him."

Catherine raised her eyebrows. "Why wouldn't you believe him?"

"Look at me. I'm as plain as a box of nails. Levy is a handsome man. He could ask any woman in this town to marry him, and stand an excellent chance she'd say yes. Why should he love someone like me?"

Catherine's voice grew stern. "Jane, stop it. You've

always doubted your worth, all because you've been comparing yourself to your friend after she married Isaac. You've got your own type of beauty, and you're nowhere near as plain as you seem to think. And Levy has worked closely with you for months now. Don't you think he's smart enough to see what's inside you?"

"I…"

"But you don't believe him."

"Maybe that's the problem. I don't believe him. I don't believe anyone like Levy would want to marry me."

"You're being a fool, Jane." Catherine's voice was firm.

The verbal slap was exactly what Jane needed. She raised her head and looked at her aunt. "Do you honestly think it's worth accepting Levy?"

"I honestly think it's worth considering. Believe it or not, *geliebte*, that may not be a bad way to start a marriage. You're good with the baby, that's why he needs you. I'm not saying you should accept his proposal, but nor should you necessarily dismiss it as hopeless. Happy marriages have been built on far less in our community."

"But unhappy marriages have been built that way too."

"*Ja*, sure. But would you truly be unhappy with Levy? He's a *gut* man."

"I agree. And I don't know." Jane stared at the floorboards at her feet, pleating the damp handkerchief, her mind churning. "I guess you're right," she said at last. "If I have any consolation, I imagine Levy is going through similar mental turmoil. And he has no one to talk it over with except a three-month-old *boppli*."

"I have no doubt that things will work out for the best, child." Catherine leaned forward and planted a kiss on Jane's forehead. "Let the matter rest with *Gott*. He'll provide the answer."

Lying in bed that night with her hands stacked beneath her head, Jane tried to pray for guidance. But in the wee hours of the night, tossing and turning and unable to sleep, Jane started questioning her personal insecurities and fears…and her reasoning took another turn.

What if she *did* accept Levy? What if she did enter into marriage, allegedly for the sake of Mercy? Was Aunt Catherine right when she said happy marriages were built on less?

Would it be so bad, being yoked to Levy? There was much to admire about him. People spoke highly of him in the community. He worked hard, was loyal and never shirked what he saw as his responsibilities.

And if he thought she was a worthwhile partner, maybe they could build a life together.

She fell asleep and dreamed Mercy was her baby… hers and Levy's.

Chapter Thirteen

Heavy-eyed, Jane stumbled over to Levy's on Monday morning. She dragged her steps, reluctant to have to think about his proposal.

Approaching Levy's house, she took a deep breath and stepped into the kitchen.

Mercy was strapped in her seat, quiet and content. Half-finished seed packets were scattered all over the table in the process of being assembled for the farmer's market. But Levy sat, his hands buried in his hair, staring at a piece of paper on the table before him. Jane's greeting died on her lips as he didn't appear to notice her at all.

The tension in the room crackled through the silence. Finally she spoke. "Levy?"

He jerked his head up, his eyes wide and startled. "What?"

His face held an extraordinary mixture of bleakness and hope, and instinct told her it came from the paper on the table.

"What's the matter?"

He looked dazed. "What?"

"What's the matter?" she repeated. "Are you *oll recht*?"

Levy remained silent a moment, then touched the paper. "I just received a letter from my sister."

"Your sister!" It was the last thing Jane expected.

"*Ja.*"

What did Eliza want after all this time? Would Levy's long-lost sister return to reclaim Mercy? She put her thoughts aside and walked into the kitchen. At least one problem was solved. Levy's marriage proposal appeared to be shelved for the moment. "So she's okay?"

"It seems so." Levy scrubbed a hand over his face. "She wants to come home."

"Home? Meaning here in Grand Creek?"

"*Ja.*"

Jane kept her voice neutral. "Then that solves one of your problems, ain't so? You won't have to pay a nanny anymore."

Levy focused on her. His eyes had dark circles under them. It appeared he'd slept no better than she had over the last couple of nights. "I owe you an apology, Jane. I stepped way over the line on Saturday, as a Christian and as a friend and as a man. It won't happen again."

Jane felt her heart break. It seems she wasn't even good enough for Levy's lame marriage proposal. Caring for babies, yes. Marriage, no.

At her silence, Levy lifted the sheet of paper. "But you're not out of a job, not yet. It will take her a while to get back. She said she anticipates being here a week from Tuesday."

"Where is she now?" Jane spoke with care, trying not to let her voice betray her emotions.

"She doesn't say, but the stamp on the envelope says Seattle."

"Seattle! So far away!"

Mercy began to whimper, and Jane guessed the baby needed her diaper changed. Glad for an excuse to leave the room, she lifted the infant out of the bouncy seat and took her into the bedroom to change her.

Eliza. Coming home. Doubtless to claim her baby. Jane took her time cleaning Mercy and putting a fresh garment on her. She slipped the baby over her shoulder and felt tears prickle her eyes at the thought of no longer having the sole care of this precious child.

"I need to get to work out in the fields," Levy called out from the kitchen. "I've already had breakfast."

"*Ja, gut.*" Jane took a deep breath and reentered the kitchen. "Do you want me to can more chutney or pie filling today?"

"If you would. I'm harvesting as fast as I can in the garden and orchard, so we'll have lots to sell on Saturday."

The work must go on. Despite the ricocheting of emotions, the work must go on.

Jane was grateful to *Gott* she hadn't said anything to Levy about her possible acceptance of his marriage proposal. It was best if those thoughts were kept to herself, to her heart alone. She drew in a deep breath, slipped Mercy into the baby sling and went to bring up more canning jars from the basement.

When Levy came in for lunch, she initiated the subject to avoid the subject of marriage. "You must be very happy your sister is coming home."

"*Ja.* And no. It's complicated."

Jane paused. "But you've done nothing but beat yourself up over her since I met you. How can you not be happy she's returning?"

"Because I don't know what she's returning from. There have been horrible situations where a *youngie* left the community, got involved in drugs or crime, then tried to return and fit in. It was often a disaster."

"But you don't think Eliza got mixed up in any of that, do you?"

He fixed his gaze on her. Then looked pointedly at the baby.

Jane bit her lip. He had a point. "Did she say anything about her circumstances in her letter?"

"*Nein*, just that she's ready to come home and be baptized." He picked at his food in silence for a few moments. Then he said, "It's going to take Eliza some time to resettle, for sure and certain."

"And she'll live here? With you?"

"*Ja*, of course. This is her home, every bit as much as mine."

Which would leave no room for the nanny. At some level, Jane realized why Eliza's return disturbed her. She was jealous.

Oh, not of the life Eliza had lived out in the *Englisch* world. Instead, Jane was jealous about the baby.

Jane would never in a million years let Levy or any-one else know how much she dreaded the thought of Eliza's return. It wasn't that Eliza would put her out of a job. She could start working at her aunt and uncle's mercantile store. But she'd grown to love Mercy, now sleeping and secure in her crib. The *boppli* was bless-edly unaware of the kaleidoscope of emotions swirling around her caregivers.

Levy returned to work. Jane concentrated on mak-ing more peach chutney for sale at the farmer's market.

By the time evening rolled around, Jane's wounded feelings were humbled as she saw how preoccupied Levy was, between news of his sister and the weekly strain of preparing for the farmer's market. Her life might be emotionally complicated, but it was nothing next to Levy's—not just concern about Mercy, but about finances and his sister's forthcoming return. He had a lot on his plate, and she didn't have to add her injured feelings on top of everything else.

By the time he sat down to dinner, he seemed more centered as well. "I think I got a lot done today," he said after the silent blessing, reaching for a bowl of green beans.

"Will Eliza be able to work the farm with you?" asked Jane. "It seems you're in desperate need of an additional pair of hands."

"*Ja*, no doubt. But I don't know what will happen when she gets here, even whether she'll want to take over Mercy's care."

Jane startled. "Surely she will. It's her daughter." She looked at little Mercy, snug in her bouncy seat in the center of the table. The infant batted at the colorful toys on the bar above her. Soon the baby would be sitting on her own, then graduating to a high chair as she learned to eat solid food. "And it won't take long to love this *boppli*."

Levy laid down his fork. "I hadn't stopped to think about that, or even how difficult this will be on you."

Jane looked down at her plate as tears stung her eyes. "It's hard not to fall for something this sweet," she admitted.

There was a short and pained silence. "I don't know what Eliza will do with Mercy," Levy warned. "She has every right to take over the care of her own child."

"Of course. But…" She looked at him with swimming eyes. "But if she does, I'll probably go to work in my uncle's store. Or go home to Ohio, back to my family. It would be too hard to see Mercy on a daily basis but not take care of her anymore."

He was silent a few minutes, eyes on his food. "Things will change after Eliza gets home, for sure and certain," he admitted. "She hasn't been here while I built up the business—the produce sales, the farmer's market, even the bookkeeping I do. I don't know what she's been doing while out in the *Englisch* world."

Jane could see why Levy had his doubts about Eliza's return.

Not wanting to offend, she just said, "It's in *Gott*'s hands. For all you know, Eliza wants to walk the straight and narrow path from now on. She could be a huge asset to the business side of things. You just don't know until she returns."

He looked troubled. "I realize that. And I aim to give her every chance—not just to settle back into the church and the community, but to help on the farm and help with the market." His mouth thinned. "But one thing I do know. It will be like having a stranger in the house again. I don't know how much she's changed, if her values are different, what her work ethic is like. I don't know her anymore, and she doesn't know me or how much I've changed. I haven't seen her in three years. That's a long time."

Her heart ached for him. She could see the love for his sister warring with the reality of his work demands. "If I may ask, Levy, why the sudden doubts? Since I've known you, you've done nothing but express regret about the mistakes you think you made in raising her. Eliza coming home is a *gut* thing, *ja*?"

"I think it's because it's now real. Now I have to deal with her."

"Don't be surprised if she's stronger and more mature than you imagine," advised Jane. "If she's been out in the *Englisch* world, it means she's changed. Hopefully any harsh experiences she had have made her grow up into a young woman of strength. In other words, don't condemn her before you see her. You might be pleasantly surprised."

Jane struggled with herself for a few minutes, then added, "But whatever happens, Levy, please don't carry a burden of guilt around anymore. Eliza is her own person. You did the best you could after your parents died, and my hope is Eliza knows that and is grateful. Besides, how many *youngies* go crazy and leave for the

Englisch world and do *schtupid* things with their lives, and who come from loving, intact homes? No one but *Gott* can change how a young person feels or behaves. Maybe *Gott* finally worked on Eliza."

"I hope so." He sighed. "I sincerely hope so."

On the walk back to her aunt and uncle's that evening, Jane reflected on her own dread of Eliza's imminent return. It was more than the possibility of losing Mercy. It was also the possibility of losing Levy. Awkward marriage proposal or not, she knew she was in love with him. But Eliza's return meant Levy's attention would be understandably divided by the needs of his sister.

In other words, she was jealous.

Maybe it was time to return to Ohio, to her parents and siblings, to her home. The emotions that had sent her fleeing here seemed eclipsed by the emotions she struggled with now.

Jane was ashamed of herself. Jealousy was an ugly emotion. She knew that from experience after watching Isaac fall in love with Hannah. The way she'd coped from that debacle was to leave Ohio and come here to Grand Creek.

Now it seemed she would be coping with her current jealousy the same way, by leaving. How could she stay and face the man who no longer even had the pretext of caring for the baby as the basis of his marriage proposal?

Once again, it seemed everything she cherished, longed for, hoped for, wished for was being snatched away. She had a moment of blazing anger at *Gott* for doing this to her...again.

She was a baptized member of the community, and her faith in *Gott* wasn't diminished. But she was angry at His hand in all this. Why couldn't Eliza have just stayed away?

The moment the thought went through her mind, she was ashamed of herself. She should be praying for Eliza's redemption, not her estrangement. Yes, jealousy was an ugly emotion.

These thoughts were not resolved by the time Jane returned to Levy's the next day. He was in the kitchen heating a bottle for Mercy. "She took a tiny bit of solid food this morning," he told her. "Eliza will be so glad she's healthy and developing normally."

"*Ja*, we must thank *Gott* Eliza will be happy." Jane heard the jealousy in her voice and turned away in shame.

Silence fell in the kitchen, and finally Levy asked, "Jane? What's the matter?"

"Nothing." To her frustration, she felt tears welling up in her eyes and refused to turn around to let Levy see them. Instead, she busied herself gathering the ingredients for making the bread she hoped to sell on Saturday.

"Are you worried about Eliza coming home?"

"*Nein*, why should I be?"

"You're not a very good liar, Jane."

She jumped, then froze when she felt his hands on her upper arms as he came up behind her. He continued gently, "I know this is hard on you, with the likelihood Eliza will take over Mercy's care. But I don't think I realized *how* hard it would be for you."

Her shoulders heaved as a sob rose in her throat. With an inarticulate sound, Levy spun her around and pulled her against his chest. Jane's pent-up emotions finally released and she burst into tears.

He stroked her back and just let her cry. A part of Jane was relieved he thought she was weeping solely over the loss of Mercy. But much of Jane's despair was the imminent loss of Levy as well—the daily interactions, the seamless work, the shared meals, the mutual concern for the baby. How long could she stay in Grand Creek if those things were no longer hers to enjoy?

The pressure of his arms and the gentle stroking on her back were too much. Not trusting her reaction to his touch, she pulled away, fished a handkerchief from her pocket and removed her glasses to mop her face. "Sorry," she murmured.

"Don't be." He stepped back. "Eliza's return will throw a wrench into a lot of things. I've been thinking it over too, and finding myself hoping she doesn't disrupt my routine to the point where I can't make a living."

"What do you mean?" She blew her nose.

"I mean, she'll need a lot of support as she transitions back into the community. I'm the logical person to give her that support. But you've also seen the tight deadlines I deal with as I prepare for each week's farmer's market. If that deadline is interrupted and I'm not ready, I don't earn money. The rest of the year I'm more flexible, but these farmer's markets bring in the bulk of my income for the year. Eliza has no idea how tight my schedule is."

In an odd way, it helped to know she wasn't alone

in realizing how much Eliza's return would complicate things. "And you said she'll be here next Tuesday?"

"*Ja.*"

"Then I will plan to not come to work that day. You and Eliza will have much to discuss."

"I'm pretty much resigned to the fact I won't get much work done that day." He glanced at the clock. "Which means I'd best get back to the fields right now."

Jane needed a huge batch of dough for bread to sell at the farmer's market. While the dough rose, she fed and changed Mercy, then slipped the baby into the sling while she did a quick once-through on housecleaning. By the time Levy came in for the evening, ten loaves of bread were cooling on racks, and she had made meat loaf with green beans for supper.

She hoped Eliza would be able to take over these tasks. Levy needed the help.

After Jane left for the day, Levy spread a small blanket on the floor and put Mercy down on her stomach so she could practice lifting her head. The *boppli* smiled readily now, and he was less clumsy with her since Jane's baby lessons were so effective.

"What will your *mamm* think of you, do you suppose?" he asked the infant. "Will she think your bumbling uncle did an okay job?"

He himself was still mulling through the ramifications of his sister's return. He recognized part of his ambivalence was wondering where Jane would fit into his life after Eliza came home.

If Eliza slipped back into the role of mother—and he

fully expected she would—where did that leave Jane? Levy realized how much he had come to look forward to seeing the woman on a daily basis. Whatever Eliza chose to do after she came home, Jane's schedule would naturally change. And Levy wasn't sure how he felt about that.

He sighed as he dangled a toy in front of Mercy. The infant raised her head and focused on it, but didn't quite have the strength or coordination to reach for it yet. That would come. She was in all ways a healthy baby, hitting all the developmental milestones she was supposed to hit—or so Jane told him. And he trusted her to know. Her gift with babies was uncanny.

She had a gift for more than babies. Since her involvement with the produce stand at the farmer's market, his income had gone up tremendously. He had just paid off the last of the hospital bills, something that would have taken him a year to do. But thanks to Jane's hard work, business sense and presence in the booth, his sales had quadrupled. And she did it all while raising a baby not her own.

He remembered looking at Jane months ago when she first came on as Mercy's nanny and thinking there was more to her than met the eye. Now that he knew her so much better, that opinion hadn't changed.

He knew beneath those thick glasses beat the heart of a warm, wonderful woman.

Chapter Fourteen

On the day before Eliza's arrival, Jane made sure Levy's house was spotless. She dusted and swept Eliza's bedroom, and made up the bed with fresh sheets and a cheerful quilt. She topped off the room's kerosene lamp and made sure the globe sparkled. She swept the house, did laundry and cleaned the kitchen.

And when Levy came in from his day's work, she hugged Mercy to her chest, kissed the child and handed her to Levy.

"Jane, wait!" he called as she marched out the front door. But she didn't answer. Instead, the tears poured from her eyes as she walked back to her aunt and uncle's house.

Feeling bleak, Levy watched Jane walk away with an air of finality that disturbed him. Mercy cooed in his arms, quiet and content, but he knew that wouldn't last as the child would soon miss the security of Jane's embrace and her confident care.

He paced around the kitchen, already missing Jane's

vivacious presence. He didn't like the way she'd left. He knew she was bothered by Eliza's upcoming return, but why couldn't she just give him a few days to get reacquainted with his sister and then get things back to normal?

He looked at the baby in his arms. What was "normal"? This whole summer had been anything but normal. He knew Jane loved Mercy very much. But would Eliza love Mercy too? Or had that bond been severed?

He sighed and put the baby in her bouncy chair, then poured himself a cup of coffee, sat down and played with the baby's toes.

"Your *mamm* is coming home," he told her. Then he wondered if that was true, or if Mercy's mother had just walked out the door. Who was Mercy's real mother?

Restless, he unstrapped Mercy and lifted her to his shoulder, then went upstairs to his sister's bedroom to get it ready. He was certain it needed dusting, and of course the bed needed to be made…

He stopped in the doorway, dumbfounded. The bedroom was pristine, with clean sheets and a bright quilt, a vase of flowers, a polished kerosene lamp on the dresser and not a particle of dust visible anywhere.

This was Jane's doing, of course. She might be filled with sorrow, but that didn't prevent her from making sure Eliza would be welcome in her own home.

He swallowed hard. Jane was a treasure. And it hit him how much he wanted to keep that treasure.

The question was, how?

Eliza arrived the following morning by taxi. She wore a blue Amish-style dress, but no apron—and no *kapp*. Her dark blond hair was pinned back in a bun, and her blue eyes were wary. She looked world-weary and cautious, as if unsure of her welcome. Above all, she looked older. During the time she'd been gone, she'd grown from a teenager into an adult.

"Eliza!" Levy rushed out the door and scooped his sister into an embrace.

Eliza hugged him tight and began to cry. "*Brüder!* I didn't know if you'd want me back."

"How could I not?" He drew back and watched the tears course down her cheeks. "This will always be your home."

"But I've been gone so long, and so many things have happened."

"Well, you're home now." He fished a clean bandanna from his pocket and handed it to her. "Come inside, we have a lot to talk about."

"Levy…" Eliza stood rooted on the side of the road. She twisted the handkerchief in her hands. "Mercy… is she okay? Is she here?"

"*Ja*, she's here. She had a good nanny while you were gone."

Eliza nodded, then followed him through the side door into the kitchen. Mercy was strapped to her bouncy seat on the table. She had reached the age where she could bat at the rod of colorful shapes above her.

"My baby," whispered Eliza. Her hands trembled as she lifted the infant out of the seat and cradled her on her shoulder. The young woman started crying again. "She's grown so much, and I've missed it all."

Levy poured two cups of coffee and led the way into

the living room, where Eliza settled into the rocking chair and cuddled the baby. Levy set one mug on the small table near her elbow.

"We have lots to discuss." He sat down in an easy chair. "First and foremost, what are your plans? You said you want to be baptized. Is it true?"

"*Ja.*" Eliza spoke without hesitation. "I want to visit the bishop tomorrow. I need to confess my sins and start the classes."

Levy closed his eyes. So *Gott* hadn't deserted him— or Eliza—after all. He opened them to see his sister cradling her child with adoration in her eyes.

"I'll have to learn to take care of you, *liebling*," she crooned to the infant. "It's been a long time since I changed your diaper, or rocked you to sleep…"

"It might be hard at first to settle back into the community," he warned. "Having an out-of-wedlock baby is…"

"Out of wedlock?" Eliza raised her head, shock on her face. "She's not out of wedlock. I was married."

It was an understatement to say Levy was surprised. "Married! Then how…"

Eliza sighed. "Let me start at the beginning. It's a long story."

She spoke nonstop for almost an hour. There was a whirlwind romance with an *Englisch* man, a hasty marriage, early pregnancy, then abrupt widowhood.

Eliza wept as she finished her story.

"When Mercy was born, I knew I couldn't care for her. Bill—that was my husband—came from a broken family, and at any rate they lived all the way across the country. I was too humiliated to return to Grand Creek. You're the only person I trusted to raise her right," she concluded, "so I sent her to you."

"It surprised me, for sure and certain," Levy admitted. "Suddenly I had a newborn arrive on my doorstep. I didn't have any idea how to take care of her, but fortunately I hired a neighbor's niece who agreed to be the baby's nanny. I realized I couldn't work and take care of Mercy at the same time."

"What kind of work are you doing? I'm completely out of touch."

While Levy filled her in on his business development for the past few years, he watched his sister's face. The tenderness with which she held her baby was a good sign.

It was only when he began explaining about Mercy's care that he understood the growing sense of unease within himself. Eliza's natural desire to care for her own child meant Jane would no longer be needed.

"…and the nanny's name is Jane," he concluded. "She's been very helpful with the farmer's market— she makes jam, bread, cookies, that kind of thing, which have sold very well."

"She sounds like a *wunderbar* nanny," observed Eliza. "And…and maybe I can find a job and help contribute to the finances."

"But then who will take care of the baby?"

Eliza flushed. "That was the problem I faced in Seattle. I couldn't work and take care of her at the same time either."

"Eliza…" Levy hesitated. "I'm glad you're home. I've

prayed to *Gott* for your redemption, and He's answered my prayers. I look forward to seeing you baptized."

He saw tears fill her eyes. "There are times I can't remember why I thought it was so important to leave. It's hard out there in the *Englisch* world. There are so many things that separate someone from their faith. My husband…" She hesitated. "He wasn't religious, and it was one of the things I most regretted the moment we were married. Despite my rebellion, I never questioned my faith. But he didn't believe in *Gott*, and his attitude started to wear me down. That's why I named this baby Mercy. I want faith always to be a part of her life."

"It's good you're back, then."

"Levy, I have to ask… Is Josiah Lapp married?"

Levy put down his mug. It was easy to see where Eliza was going with this train of thought. "*Nein*. Not yet, at least. He's been courting a young woman, though, so I wouldn't get your hopes up."

"I won't. Still, I… I want to see Josiah, to apologize. I know he thought about me as part of his future, and I ruined that. I won't interfere with whomever he's courting, of course, but he's been on my conscience."

"You'll see him on Church Sundays."

"*Ja*, but it's not like we'll have much of a chance to talk privately. Or rather, I'll understand if he avoids me."

"Then maybe you should just ask him if you can meet later on. But Eliza, you need to make good choices from now on."

"*Ja*, I plan to." She bit her lip. "Sometimes I think how different my life would have been had Josiah and I gotten married, if I'd stayed behind and accepted a quiet, calm life instead of one filled with drama and angst. Why I ever thought drama and angst were preferable to peace, I don't know."

"You really *have* grown up, little *schweschder*." He smiled.

"I didn't have much of a choice." She kept her eyes on the baby. "But now I have to find work. Maybe we should keep the nanny so I can look for a job?"

"Maybe we should. She's been a blessing. I don't know what I would have done without her."

Eliza peered at him closely. "That sounds like more than just professional gratitude."

"It might be." He didn't deny it. "She's amazing with the baby, she's amazing in the home and the garden and the farmer's market. She's an amazingly hard worker. She's also kind and generous and funny."

"So my big *brüder* has fallen in love at last." Eliza smiled through her tears.

In love? Levy froze. With blinding clarity, he realized his sister was right.

Jane, with her glasses that always fell down her nose. Jane, caring for Mercy with a competency that came naturally. Jane, teaching him what he needed to know to tend to the infant. Jane, making bread and cookies and jams to sell. Jane, shoring him up whenever he was down.

He felt dazed he hadn't recognized this before. His eyes unfocused as he realized how much he had come to love the tall, gawky woman who had saved him when Mercy arrived. "*Ja*," he said slowly. "I think I have." His heart started pounding. "I don't think I realized just how much I loved her until now." A grin spread across his face.

"Does she return the sentiment?"

His smile was wiped away as he recounted his clumsy marriage proposal from ten days before. "I don't know."

"Then you need to find out. After *Mamm* and *Daed* died, you put your life on hold to finish raising me. I paid you back by rebelling and running away. As a result, I missed out on a great many things, including raising my child." She hugged Mercy closer. "I also missed out on marrying Josiah. Don't make the same mistakes I did. It's okay to admit you love this woman. If that's the case, you need to let her know."

"I need to think on this." He still felt dazed at the realization of his feelings for Jane. "I need to figure out what to do…"

"What is there to figure out? If you love her, then court her. Just don't wait too long."

"So now my baby *schweschder* is advising me?" Levy beamed.

"Your baby *schweschder* has been a fool her whole life." Eliza smiled through tears. "If I can keep even one person from making a bad decision, then it will make me happy. If you love this woman, don't let her get away."

Jane rattled around her aunt and uncle's store, restocking shelves and trying not to obsess about what was happening in the Struder home. Would Eliza want to care for her own baby? Jane assumed she would. If that was the case, she certainly was out of a job.

She realized there was something she could do: pack.

She would ask Uncle Peter to take her to the train station tomorrow. She had told Levy she would stay until the farmer's market season ended at the end of October, but things had changed now that Eliza was home. If she left, she wouldn't have to bear the pain of watching Mercy back with her mother. Nor would she have to see Levy, who could now concentrate on rebuilding his family. Yes, it was better if she left.

"So you're serious about going home, then?" asked Aunt Catherine that evening as Jane helped wash the supper dishes.

"*Ja*, I think it best."

"Is it Eliza?"

Jane nodded. "I assume she wants to raise her own baby, in which case I'd only be in the way."

"You could work with us in the store."

"And see Mercy on Church Sundays but know she's not mine?" Pain shot through her at the thought. "And you know how I feel about Levy. I… I can't bear to be around either of them if…" Her voice trailed off and she blinked back tears.

"I'm sorry it didn't work out, *liebling*."

At her aunt's gentle tone, a single tear rolled down Jane's cheek. She wiped it away and dried another plate. "It seems *Gott* hasn't decided what to do with me yet. Maybe I'll find the answer back home in Ohio."

"I know you don't want to hear this, Jane, but I think you should talk things over with Levy before you go."

"Why? What can he possibly say? 'Stay because you're *useful*'? No. I won't have it."

"So you intend to just leave without explanation?"

"It sounds rude, but I think it's best. I can always send him a letter later on, but for now, I don't want to see him. Or Eliza."

"I think you might be turning Eliza into a bigger problem than she really is."

"She's Mercy's mother. That's not a problem, that's a fact. I'm not needed anymore." She spoke in a tight, controlled voice.

"You're always needed, Jane." Catherine's voice was gentle.

Jane felt ashamed. She leaned over and kissed her aunt on the cheek. "You and Onkel Peter have been so good to me. I honestly didn't expect to fall in love with anyone while here in Grand Creek, but that's what happened. But Levy never looked at me as a woman. Even his offer of marriage was based purely on his need for a permanent nanny. Everything has changed with Eliza's return, and I can't stay here when I'd be seeing Levy daily and knowing I'm not even *useful* to him anymore."

Catherine sighed. "Well if you're sure, I'll let Peter know. I'm sure he can take you to the train station tomorrow."

"*Danke*, Tante Catherine." Jane put away the last dish. "I'll go finish packing."

Wednesday dawned bright and sunny, with a hint of a breeze and a promise of a beautiful autumn day. Levy bent over the tomato plants in the field, trying not to wonder where Jane was. He worked methodically, filling baskets with ripe tomatoes. He would transfer the tomatoes to crates and stack them in the cool dark basement until the Saturday market.

Jane's absence preyed on his mind. With Eliza home, it was obvious Jane was staying away. He told his sister she was probably working at her aunt and uncle's store.

Eliza had walked over to talk with the bishop. She also told him she wanted to visit the Troyers' store to meet and thank Jane.

He looked up as Eliza came walking through the garden rows, carrying Mercy over one shoulder. "How did your meeting with the bishop go?"

"It went well. Better than I hoped, in fact. I told him everything that happened since I left Grand Creek." She patted the baby's back. "In some ways I think he was relieved to know about the circumstances around Mercy's birth. Most importantly, he's going to put up the possibility of my baptism to a church vote. If the decision is unanimous, I'll start classes toward baptism."

"*Ach*, that's *gut*. The bishop is a fair man. I'm glad he's working with you on this."

"Also, I stopped by the Troyers' store and had a talk with Catherine Troyer. She's willing to have me work in the store if I can figure out who can take care of Mercy."

"Won't Jane do it? I have a feeling she'd be more than happy to continue caring for her."

"Jane's gone. Catherine said Peter is taking her to the train station—"

"What!" Levy jerked upright and the basket tipped over. Crimson tomatoes rolled away. "What did you say? Jane's gone?"

"*Ja*. I wanted to thank her for taking care of Mercy,

but Catherine said Peter had left about an hour before. I guess she's returning to Ohio."

Levy stood frozen, frantic thoughts racing through his mind. He felt stunned by the loss.

"Levy, what's the matter?"

"She can't go. She can't." His lips felt cold, his hands numb. The thought of not having Jane nearby made him realize just how much she meant to him. Why had he never said anything to her? Why had he left her in doubt as to his feelings? Without question she felt he'd just moved beyond needing her now that Eliza was home. "She *can't* go," he repeated in shock.

"But she's on her way home. Levy…" Eliza reached out and touched his arm. "Are you that much in love with her?"

"*Ja.*" He refused to admit how close to tears he felt. "Why did she leave so quickly? Why didn't she let me know she planned to leave?"

"Sounds like you two need to talk."

"How can we talk if she's already at the train station?" snapped Levy, glaring at his sister.

But the young woman smiled with the wisdom of hard knocks. "But she's *not* at the train station. Not yet. If Peter's been gone only an hour by this point, then they still have some distance to go…"

"…and I might be able to catch up with them." Suddenly sure, Levy yanked off his gloves, dropped them to the ground and sprinted toward the barn.

Chapter Fifteen

Levy wanted Jane. He needed her. These last few months of daily contact cemented how strongly his feelings toward her had grown.

His favorite mare was a former harness racer, able to achieve high speeds at a trotting pace. Levy had never considered the animal's pedigree very impressive before, but today he blessed her heritage.

As he urged his horse to pull the buggy faster, he regretted his clumsy marriage proposal of a couple weeks earlier. What was he thinking, destroying her hopes for a stable loving partnership by pitching nothing more than a convenient business arrangement? Convenient to him, perhaps, but insulting to her.

How she felt about him, he wasn't quite sure. He'd pushed her patience more than she deserved, taken advantage of her skills and talents in creating items to sell at the farmer's market, without considering the workload he'd placed on her. In all ways, he'd taken her for granted. And now he might be paying the ultimate price—losing her—if he didn't catch up with her in time.

An Amish buggy loomed ahead. Levy pulled up alongside, but it proved to belong to Eli Herschberger, his graying beard forking in the breeze. "In a hurry!" he called to the older man, flourishing a hand and urging his horse to higher speeds.

If he failed to catch up with Peter's buggy, if Jane departed on the train before he had a chance to explain, what would he do? He realized he wanted nothing more than Jane at his side for the rest of his life. But first he had some apologizing to do.

As they sat in the buggy together, Jane's uncle told her, "You are loved, child, never forget that."

"*Ja, danke.* I know." She touched his arm. "But sometimes the love of relatives or even the love of children simply isn't enough."

Uncle Peter sighed. "Well, our home is always open if you ever change your mind and want to come back…"

A car raced past them, just one of many on this busy road as they got nearer to the train station.

"I forget how noisy it is here." Jane shook her head. "I'll be glad to get back to Ohio and see *Mamm* and *Daed.*"

"Your aunt and I were discussing who we might hire in the store," remarked Peter. "We thought perhaps Eliza might be interested."

"Levy's sister?"

"*Ja*, sure. Why wouldn't she work for us? She needs a job."

"But who will take care of the baby?"

Peter rubbed his chin. "I don't know if that's been solved, so perhaps it won't work out after all. But Catherine's minding the store by herself right now, and as I'm sure you're aware from working the farmer's market with Levy, it's tough working solo."

Jane frowned. "And she's alone because you're taking the time to drive me to the station…"

He patted her hand. "I'm glad to do it, niece."

But Jane wasn't placated. Her sigh was both bitter and frustrated. "It seems I have a habit of sowing problems and discontent wherever I go."

"You do nothing of the sort. For the time you were here, you solved a great problem. It just wasn't *our* problem, true, but you helped Levy when he badly needed it."

"And now he doesn't need me anymore—" She broke off, startled to hear fast-approaching hoofbeats behind them.

Uncle Peter directed his horse to a wide spot off the road to make room for the passing buggy, but instead the vehicle slowed down and came alongside them. Jane peered around the corner and her jaw dropped. "Levy!"

He called "Whoa!" To the panting horse and pulled the animal to a stop as Uncle Peter did the same.

"Jane, I need to talk to you."

Her face shuttered. "Why? What is there to say?"

"You won't know until you hear, right?"

"I'm on my way home to Ohio."

"*Ja*, I know. But you're not going."

Her mouth thinned. "You have no right to tell me what I can and cannot do."

"You're right, I don't. Then let me ask. *Please* don't go." He climbed out of the buggy and approached her.

"What are you doing?"

"Asking your uncle if he'll be kind enough to let me drive you home."

"Levy, I have my plans."

"*Ja*, you probably do. But you haven't heard *my* plans."

Something in the tone of his voice made her pause.

"I certainly wouldn't mind getting back to the store," Uncle Peter said to Jane. "Your aunt is working by herself."

Jane sighed and climbed out of the buggy, taking Levy's outstretched hand as she stepped down.

"Thank you, Peter," Levy said. "I'll bring her back."

Uncle Peter turned his horse around, crossed the street and headed back toward Grand Creek.

"What's this all about?" asked Jane. She tried to deny the searing hope that trembled at the edge of her soul. Why had Levy run after her? Why had he stopped her plans to return home?

"I need to let Maggie rest a bit." Levy gestured toward a nearby park with generous shade trees and a hitching post for Amish buggies. "Will you let me rest her?"

"Of course." Avoiding him, she turned and patted the animal's sweating neck.

Leading the horse, Levy walked toward the cool

oasis. Jane, silent but with her emotions in chaos, walked on the other side of the mare.

Levy hitched the animal to the hitching post and sat down on a bench. Jane perched at the other end.

"I…" His voice came out as a croak, and he cleared his throat. "I have to apologize," he began.

"For what?"

"For many things, but first and foremost for that clumsy marriage proposal I made a couple weeks ago. I've been beating myself up over it ever since."

Jane's emotions cooled. Is that what this was all about? "You already apologized, remember? You're forgiven."

"*Nein*, I'm not. I don't deserve to be. I've had a hard time in the past, forgiving myself. I spent so many years taking on the blame for what Eliza did. But where you're concerned, I don't want to look ahead to years of regret. I can't mess this up again. I can't let you go, Jane."

Her heart began hammering. Levy was still being awkward and clumsy in some ways. But he was trying very hard to say something very important. Above all, Jane did not want to misunderstand his intent. "What do you mean?"

"Jane…" He groped for her hands, held them firmly in his. "I want to ask you again to be my wife. Not as a business arrangement, not as a permanent nanny to Mercy, but because I love you."

Her jaw dropped open in shock. She spent a few moments simply gaping at him. "Levy, where did this come from? I thought you didn't like me."

"Didn't like you!" He stared. "Nothing could be

further from the truth! Jane, I've worked with you for months now, and everything you do is wonderful. Everything. Your wit, your intelligence, your dedication to Mercy, your business sense, your hard work—everything. I haven't found anything about you I couldn't admire. It was only when Eliza told me you were going home that I realized how much I loved you."

Conflicting emotions warred within her. This change of feeling on his part was so sudden, so unexpected, that she didn't know what to say. For one of the few times in her life, she was speechless.

At her silence, she saw panic cloud Levy's face. "Please, Jane, say yes."

"I…I…" she stuttered.

His grip tightened on her hands, then he released them and half turned away. "So I misread the situation." He dropped his head in his hands in despair. "I embarrassed you again with my clumsiness. I'm so sorry."

"Levy, this is all so unexpected," Jane choked out. "I was going home because I was convinced I meant nothing to you…"

He raised his head. "You mean the world to me, Jane. You mean the moon and the stars to me."

She couldn't help but smile a bit at his melodramatic turns of phrase. Then she turned serious. "Levy, what about your sister? What about Mercy?"

"I don't know yet. She seems anxious to become a mother to her own child, but she'll need help. She talked to your aunt about working in the store…"

"But if she works in the store, what about the baby? Who's going to take care of her?"

"That's part of the problem. She wants to contribute, but doesn't quite know how. Jane, there's something else you should know. Mercy wasn't born out of wedlock. Eliza was married to an *Englischer*, but he died in a car accident while she was pregnant."

Jane gasped. "*Ach*, how sad!"

He closed his eyes and pinched the bridge of his nose. "It's very complicated. She has a long road ahead of her, but at least she wants to stay and be baptized."

"Then *Gott* did answer your prayers."

"*Ja*, as far as Eliza is concerned." He looked at her. "I'm still waiting to see if He answers my prayers as far as you're concerned. I'm waiting to see if Mercy's beautiful nanny will become my wife."

Maybe it was the hand of *Gott* reaching out, but she suddenly felt more confident of her path.

But she warned him, "I can be stubborn and hot tempered…"

"Welcome to the club."

She laughed at that. "Levy… I… I have a confession to make. I thought about accepting your marriage proposal a couple weeks ago until the letter from your sister changed things."

He couldn't have looked more surprised than if she'd clobbered him over the head. "But you turned me down!"

"*Ja*, with some hotheaded words, as I recall. But later I talked things over with Tante Catherine. I thought about it all through the night and decided a one-sided marriage could eventually be made to work."

"One-sided? You mean…?"

"*Ja.* I fell in love with you a long time ago, Levy. But I felt you didn't see me as a marriageable woman, just a *useful* one." Her old bitterness still tinged the word. "I couldn't seem to escape the curse of being *useful* but not *lovable.*"

A tremulous smile lit his face. "So…has *Gott* answered my prayers?"

"*Ja.* I will marry you, Levy."

Epilogue

"It's lovely." Aunt Catherine laid out Jane's blue dress. "Eliza did a beautiful job sewing it."

"I feel a little guilty, not sewing my own wedding dress." Jane fingered the dark blue fabric which, she knew, brought out the color of her eyes. "But Eliza is such a fine seamstress, and she really wanted to make the dress. I think it's one of her ways to thank me for taking care of Mercy for her."

"Eliza has certainly settled down. I'm glad she's one of your wedding *newehockers*."

"And my younger sisters are the other two attendants."

"Your parents seem to like Levy very much. I'm so glad." Catherine dropped a kiss on Jane's forehead. "You and Levy will be very happy, I'm sure."

Jane hugged herself, her face aglow. "It's a dream come true. I should have known *Gott* had a plan for me. And Levy. And Eliza. And Mercy."

Catherine chuckled. "I must say, you make one of

the happiest brides I've ever seen. And by this time to-morrow, you and Levy will be bound forever." Cath-erine's eyes crinkled. "You're both *gut* for each other, that I can plainly see."

"She's *gut* for me," said Levy, coming into the room.

"No doubts about your future wife?" teased Cath-erine.

"Are you kidding? *Gott* gave me the most beautiful bride in the world."

Jane felt her heart well up with love for this man who thought her beautiful.

Aunt Catherine looked from one to the other, then murmured, "I think I hear Peter calling me," and es-caped from the room.

"Tomorrow." Levy smiled at her.

"Tomorrow," breathed Jane.

Just after noon on the following day, Bishop Kemp stood before the gathered community and concluded his sermon on the merits of marriage.

"Levy and Jane, please come forward," intoned the bishop.

Attired in her new blue dress, Jane stood up and faced the leader of their community. Beside her, Levy also stood.

"You have heard the ordinance of wedlock within the provisions of our faith," Bishop Kemp said. "Are you now willing to enter wedlock together as *Gott* in the beginning ordained and commanded?"

Levy spoke first. "*Ja.*"

Jane spoke next. "*Ja.*"

The bishop directed his next words to Levy. "Do you stand in the confidence that this, our sister, is ordained of *Gott* to be your wedded wife?"

"*Ja.*"

The bishop turned to her. "Do you stand in the confidence that this, our brother, is ordained of *Gott* to be your wedded husband?"

Ordained of Gott. Never were there truer words. This man to whom she was joining herself was, indeed, ordained by *Gott.* Jane fought back tears. "*Ja.*"

The bishop continued with the vows. Then he took her right hand and clasped it with Levy's. His grip was strong, sure, confident. Jane smiled up at the man now joined with her for the rest of her life.

"...be with you and help you together and fulfill His blessing abundantly upon you through Jesus Christ. *Amein,*" concluded the bishop. He wiped a tear away and smiled at the couple.

She looked at Levy, the strong, handsome man who had chosen her—a plain Jane—as his wife. Above all, she wanted to lean in and kiss him, but that wasn't done at a wedding ceremony. Instead, she turned her attention to the bishop for the closing formalities.

Levy's hand was warm around hers. She was now something she never thought she would be—Levy's wife—and she closed her eyes a moment. "*Danke, Gott,*" she whispered.

"*Ja,*" Levy whispered back. His hand tightened over hers. "*Danke.*"

* * * * *

If you enjoyed this book by Patrice Lewis,
be sure to pick up
The Amish Newcomer

And check out these other Amish stories

A Secret Amish Crush *by Marta Perry.*
Someone to Trust *by Patricia Davids.*
Her Forbidden Amish Love *by Jocelyn McClay.*

Available now from Love Inspired!

Find more great reads at
www.LoveInspired.com

Tante Catherine's Macaroni and Cheese

1 pound pasta (spiral or elbow macaroni).
1 cube (8 tablespoons) butter or margarine.
1 cup flour.
1 teaspoon salt.
½ teaspoon pepper.
½ teaspoon onion powder.
4 cups milk.
2 ½ cups shredded Cheddar cheese.
2 teaspoons ground mustard.
1 teaspoon Worcestershire sauce.

For topping:
½ cup Parmesan cheese.
½ cup breadcrumbs.

Directions

Preheat oven to 400°F.

Add pasta to large pot of boiling water (with ½ teaspoon salt, if desired); cook for about eight minutes. Turn off heat, drain pasta, return to pot.

In a large saucepan, melt butter at low heat. Stir in flour a tablespoon at a time while drizzling in milk to make a white sauce. Once all the milk is added, cook at low heat, stirring constantly, until sauce thickens. Turn off heat. Add spices, Worcestershire sauce and cheese, stir until cheese melts.

Pour cheese sauce over pasta, stir to coat.

Pour pasta/cheese into 9x13 Pyrex baking dish (or other three-quart oven baking dish). Sprinkle with Parmesan/breadcrumb topping. Bake, uncovered, for 20 minutes or until topping is lightly browned.

Dear Reader,

I hope you've enjoyed reading Jane and Levy's story. This book meant a lot to me because I, too, am a plain Jane. And I, too, met my "Levy" and have been blessed with thirty wonderful years of marriage to my best friend, a man who looked past my face and saw my heart.

During all our years together, we've operated a home woodcraft business. While we've never run a booth at a farmer's market, we've run just about every other kind of booth you can imagine. We also have a small farm where we raise similar produce to what Levy raises. In short, there's a lot of personal experience in these pages!

I love hearing from readers and welcome emails at patricelewis@hotmail.com.

Patrice

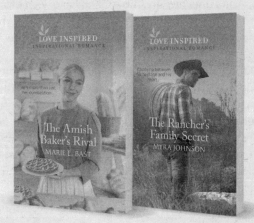

COMING NEXT MONTH FROM
Love Inspired

Available March 30, 2021

THE BABY NEXT DOOR
Indiana Amish Brides • by Vannetta Chapman
When Grace Troyer and her baby girl move back home, the Amish bachelor next door can't resist the little family. But Adrian Schrock's plan to nudge Grace out of her shell by asking her to cook for *Englischers* on his farm tour might just expose secrets Grace hopes to keep buried...

THE AMISH TEACHER'S WISH
by Tracey J. Lyons
With the school damaged during a storm, teacher Sadie Fischer needs Levi Byler's help repairing it. As they work together, Levi's determined he *won't* become a part of her search for a husband. But Sadie might be the perfect woman to mend his heart...and convince him forever isn't just for fairy tales.

REBUILDING HER LIFE
Kendrick Creek • by Ruth Logan Herne
Home to help rebuild her mother's clinic after a forest fire, Jess Bristol never expects Shane Stone—the man she once wrongfully sent to jail—to arrive with the same purpose. But as sparks fly between them and she falls for the children in his care, can their troubled past lead to a happy future?

A TRUE COWBOY
Double R Legacy • by Danica Favorite
The last thing William Bennett ever thought he'd do was plan a benefit rodeo, but it's the perfect way to move on after his ex-fiancée's betrayal. But his partner on the project, single and pregnant Grace Duncan, is scaling the walls around his heart...with a secret that could destroy their budding love.

HER SECRET HOPE
by Lorraine Beatty
With her life and career in tatters, journalist Melody Williams takes a job working on a book about the history of a small town—and discovers her boss is the father of the child she gave up. Clay Reynolds secretly adopted their little boy, but can he trust Melody with the truth...and their son?

THEIR FAMILY ARRANGEMENT
by Angel Moore
After they lose their best friends in a tragic accident, former high school sweethearts Kevin Lane and Sophie Owens will do anything to keep the two orphaned children left in their custody. So when a judge insists on a couple to parent the children, a temporary engagement is the only solution...

LOOK FOR THESE AND OTHER LOVE INSPIRED BOOKS WHEREVER BOOKS ARE SOLD, INCLUDING MOST BOOKSTORES, SUPERMARKETS, DISCOUNT STORES AND DRUGSTORES.

LICNM0321

Get 4 FREE REWARDS!

We'll send you 2 FREE Books plus 2 FREE Mystery Gifts.

Love Inspired books feature uplifting stories where faith helps guide you through life's challenges and discover the promise of a new beginning.

FREE Value Over **$20**

Grace found Nicole had pulled herself up to the front door and was high-fiving none other than Adrian Schrock. He'd squatted down to her level. Nicole was having a fine old time.

Grace picked up her *doschder* and pushed open the door, causing Adrian to jump up, then step back toward the porch steps. It was, indeed, a fine spring day. The sun shone brightly across the Indiana fields. Flowers colored yellow, red, lavender and orange had begun popping through the soil that surrounded the porch. Birds were even chirping merrily.

Somehow, all those things did little to elevate Grace's mood. Neither did the sight of her neighbor.

Adrian resettled his straw hat on his head and smiled. *"Gudemariye."*

"Your llama has escaped again."

"Kendrick? *Ya.* I've come to fetch him. He seems to like your place more than mine."

"I don't want that animal over here, Adrian. He spits. And your peacock was here at daybreak, crying like a child."

Adrian laughed. "When you moved back home, I guess you didn't expect to live next to a Plain & Simple Exotic Animal Farm."

Adrian wiggled his eyebrows at Nicole when he seemed to realize that Grace wasn't amused.

"I think of your place as Adrian's Zoo."

"Not a bad name, but it doesn't highlight our Amish heritage enough."

"The point is that I feel like we're living next door to a menagerie of animals."

"Up, Aden. Up."

Adrian scooped Nicole from Grace's hold, held her high above his head, then nuzzled her neck. Adrian was comfortable with everyone and everything.

"Do you think she'll ever learn to say my name right?"

"Possibly. Can you please catch Kendrick and take him back to your place?"

"Of course. That's why I came over. I guess I must have left the gate open again." He kissed Nicole's cheek, then popped her back into Grace's arms. "You should bring her over to see the turtles."

As he walked away, Grace wondered for the hundredth time why he wasn't married. It was true that he'd picked a strange profession. What other Amish man raised exotic animals? No, Adrian wouldn't be considered excellent marrying material by most young Amish women.

Don't miss
The Baby Next Door *by Vannetta Chapman,*
available April 2021 wherever
Love Inspired books and ebooks are sold.

LoveInspired.com

LIEXP0321